MW01041980

Please find me...

Ghost of the Overlook

Diane Stringam Tolley

Please find me...

Ghost
of the
Overlook

Diane Stringam Tolley

Summary: Tabitha Pillay and her parents move into a grand old hotel, then discover it is haunted by a small spirit that needs Tabby's help.

ISBN- 13-978-1533608956
ISBN-10: 1533608954

Cover design © 2016 by Diane Stringam Tolley
Edited by Caitlin Clark
Cover Photo by tobkatrina

Ghost is dedicated to:
Megan, Kyra, Erini, Bronwyn,
Linnea, Hazel, Willow and Leah.
And all those who, like them, enjoy being
'just a little bit scared'!

Chapter 1: Where Tabby Finds Herself and Her Parents Starting Over. At the Overlook.

Tabby flipped her long, blonde braid behind her shoulder and kicked at the gravel in the drive. "I don't care what you say," she said. "I *hate* it here! I've waited *forever* for Mr. Bauer's grade six class with Cassie and Laurie."

Her mother pursed her lips, scratched the back of her neck and stared at her tall, determined daughter.

Her dad sighed and shrugged and walked around to the back of the car. "Well, maybe you won't feel that way after you've been here for a while."

Tabby rolled her eyes and looked up at the hotel that jutted over them like a mountain with peaked roofs, turrets and strange little outcroppings. Banks of windows looked down on them like silver, staring eyes.

She shivered. "I don't think so," she said, her voice a little softer. "It looks—spooky."

Something moved on one of the little roofs and Tabby's eyes darted instinctively toward it. Her eyes widened as she realized that someone was there, standing still and erect on that steeply pitched surface.

Someone wearing a long, white—dress.

The figure turned toward them and Tabby felt the hairs on the back of her neck stand up. She shivered again. Who on earth would be standing there on the roof of the hotel? Could it be a guest—or a worker? She shook her head. No worker would be dressed like that. And whoever it was, they were standing on a distinctly unsafe surface.

She shifted closer to her parents. "Mom, Dad, look up there!" she said, pointing.

"What is it, Tabs?" her dad asked as he lifted a suitcase from the back of the car.

"There's—"

Just then, they all heard the distinct crunch of someone's feet in the gravel.

Tabby spun around as a small, slender, elderly man approached them, his hand outstretched. "Ah," he said. "Our new hotel manager. Welcome, Mr. Pillay."

Tabby frowned at the man doubtfully. His words sounded welcoming, but his expression was anything but.

All the lines in his pasty-white face drooped like a tall, straight candle melting in the heat. A few strands of wispy hair clung to the top of his head and slightly bulging, dark eyes, further magnified by thick glasses, looked as though they had been poked hastily into his soft, doughy skin.

Tabby's dad, tall, lean and white-haired, towered over the man. The two shook hands. "Call me David," he said. "And thank you, Mr. Withers."

Mr. Withers nodded and turned to Tabby's mom. "And this is your wife?"

"It is," Tabby's dad said. "My wife, Rose."

"Ah. Rose." Mr. Withers offered her his hand.

"And our daughter, Tabitha."

"Tabitha." This time, the man didn't offer his hand, but merely looked intently at her with those weird eyes.

Finally he nodded slightly in her direction and, turning, indicated that they should follow him. "Come," he said. "Leave your bags. Oscar will take them up to your suite while you take the tour."

Obediently, Tabby's parents trailed along behind.

Tabby stopped for a moment to study the rooftop again, but the figure in white was no longer visible. She hurried to catch up to the others.

Mr. Withers led them to the massive front doors. "Welcome to the Overlook Hotel," he said, throwing them open dramatically.

Tabby and her parents stepped past him and onto thick carpets.

After the bright sunlight outside, Tabby had to wait a moment for her eyes to adjust to the gloom of the lobby. It was massive, taking up one whole side of the hotel, and ineffectively lit by the banks of windows on two sides.

2

She looked up to the high ceiling where wooden beams crisscrossed, forming a giant spider's web of lines. Great wood and brass light fixtures, unlit in the afternoon sunlight, hung from long chains attached to those beams.

Heavy, carved tables and chairs and assorted furniture were set in little haphazard groupings about the room. An enormous staircase curved up from the centre of the room to the second floor and ended at a wide balcony that hung over the floor below.

The lobby desk, across from the front entrance and partially hidden by the staircase, ran half the length of the room. There were three people standing behind it, two waiting on guests and one writing something in a book.

The third person, a slender woman with short, red hair, looked up, closed her book and came out from behind the desk towards them. "You must be the new Manager," she said, offering Tabby's dad her hand.

"Mr. Pillay," Mr. Withers broke in. "And this is his family. Rose," he indicated. "And Tabitha."

"I'm David," Tabby's dad said.

"Jana," the woman said. "The Assistant Manager."

Tabby looked at her. She was smiling, but, like Mr. Withers, there was something funny about that smile.

"Very nice to finally get to meet you, Jana," David said. "I've heard lots of good things about you."

"Not good enough, obviously." Jana's smile slipped somewhat and she glanced briefly sideways at Mr. Withers.

"I have suggested that the Pillays have a tour," Mr. Withers said. "Jana, if you would be so kind—" his voice trailed off as he waved a hand, then he turned abruptly and walked away.

"Well, I guess it's up to me," Jana said, her smile back in place.

"Lead on," Tabby's dad said.

Jana nodded, then led them toward the staircase. "Best place to start is at the top."

For the next hour, Jana showed them through a tangle of hallways, guest suites, swimming pools, banquet, exercise and meeting rooms, storage closets, kitchens and laundries.

3

Throughout, she and Tabby's dad talked steadily. Stats, routines, schedules, problems, and maintenance, but Tabby tuned them out, concentrating instead on creating a map in her head.

Finally, they were back on the main floor where Jana led them to a large pair of doors further along the wall from the great front desk. "And this," she said, "is the famous Overlook Ballroom." She threw the doors back with a flourish.

A sigh of wind, smelling strangely of blossoms and dust, blew past them and Tabby shivered suddenly.

"Oh, this is lovely," Tabby's mom said, stepping through.

Tabby's feet lagged as she followed her parents into the cavernous room. For some reason, she felt reluctant to go in and she stopped as soon as she had barely cleared the doorway and looked around.

For someone used to living in hotels, it looked ordinary enough with its great long room, chandeliers wrapped in fine net to keep bugs and dust away, and white drapes over the few pieces of furniture.

But for some reason, it 'felt' different.

She glanced at her parents but they didn't seem to have noticed anything strange. Indeed, they had walked out onto the dance floor where Tabby's mom spun around in a circle, arms outstretched. "Oh, David, this is lovely!" she said.

Tabby drifted forward as her dad laughed at her mother and caught one of her hands. "Dance with me, Rose," he said, sweeping his wife into his arms.

"Oh, David, you've got to be careful," her mom cautioned.

"Nonsense! Dance with me, woman!" He began to hum a waltz and the two of them spun gracefully across the floor.

Before her dad's illness, the two of them had done a lot of dancing and Tabby realized now that she had missed watching them. She smiled as they moved about the room, their heads close together; her dad's prematurely white, and her mom's long blonde braid.

There was a bank of dark mirrors opposite and Tabby could see the reflection of two figures flowing together across the dance floor.

4

Suddenly, she frowned as she noticed a third, very faint figure which seemed to be moving along behind them in the mirror.

Her heart beginning to beat a little faster, Tabby glanced around. Jana was standing where they had left her, watching the dancing couple, and there was no one else in the room.

Tabby turned back to the mirror and looked into it intently, immediately spotting Jana's reflection and her own.

She again looked towards her parents, blissfully waltzing their way across the ballroom. The third figure was still there. Though it was faint, Tabby could clearly see it moving and spinning along just behind her parents.

Just then, Jana cleared her throat and instantly, the figure vanished.

Tabby stared at the spot where it had been. Had she imagined it? She closed her eyes. The lighter figure showed up clearly against her closed lids.

She turned back toward her parents. "Dad—" she began. Then she stopped. What could she say?

Tabby's dad dipped her mom and spun her around one last time. "Duty calls," he sighed.

Her mom giggled and the two of them walked back to Jana.

"Sorry, Jana," Tabby's dad said. "It was too tempting to be missed."

Jana smiled slightly. "So you have been ill?" she asked.

He frowned slightly and nodded. "Cancer," he said. "But I'm in remission now."

Jana studied him. "Really."

"Yes," Tabby's mom spoke up. "It was touch and go for a while, but the doctors are very happy with him."

"I'm tough," her dad said, grinning.

"Was that why you gave up your last job?" Jana said.

His grin disappeared.

"If you don't mind my asking," Jana added belatedly.

"It's no secret," he said, sighing. "I was General Manager at the Fairmont Banff Springs Hotel in Banff, Alberta and my illness forced me to give up my post."

"It's been rough," Tabby's mom said. "The doctors gave him a clean bill of health two months ago but he's been looking for work for a while now."

"Finding this opportunity was quite literally an answer to prayer," her dad said.

"Yes, well—" Jana said, wrinkling her nose slightly, "—if you've seen all there is to see here—" she turned and led the way back to the doors.

Tabby's parents looked at each other and her dad raised his eyebrows. "I'm really very grateful for the job, Jana," he said quietly, following behind the woman. "I'll be relying on you to guide me for the first little while."

"I'm sure you will," Jana said.

She reached the doors and turned toward them. "I understand that you've been very ill, Mr. Pillay," she said. "And I don't mean to be—difficult, but we need to know that you can handle things here."

Tabby's dad looked at her. "I've 'handled' things in a good many hotels. Even before I worked my way up to the Banff Springs job."

Jana was watching him. "I understand that, Mr. Pillay. But this hotel is a bit different from most hotels."

"In what way—"

She cut him off. "Because, you see, this hotel happens to be haunted."

Chapter 2: Another Haunted Hotel. Sigh.

"You knew? All this time, you knew?" Tabby's mom was holding a white sweater she had just pulled from her suitcase.

"Of course I did, hon," Tabby's dad said. He shrugged. "I just didn't think much about it."

"Didn't think—" her mom snorted and marched to the closet.

Jana had shown Tabby and her parents to their new apartment. Now Tabby, sitting on the bench at the foot of her parents' bed, was watching them unpack.

Her dad walked over and caught her mom by the shoulders. "Rose, think about it," he said. "A haunted hotel? How many hotels in the world make that same claim?"

Her mom turned to face him. Finally, she shrugged. "A lot?"

"Exactly! Most of them, in fact. Why, even the Banff Springs claimed to have its resident ghosts."

"That's right," Tabby spoke up. "The ghost on the seventh floor." Tabby and her friends had spent every hour of their free time trying to catch a glimpse of the elusive spirit. They had been such fun times. She frowned as she thought again about the faint figure in the ballroom. Ghost hunting was much less 'shivery' when you had your friends with you.

Her mom smiled slightly. "Well, I wish you would have mentioned something."

"Sorry, hon," Tabby's dad hugged her. "I guess I may as well tell you that I think the reason I got this job is because of the stories of a resident ghost."

Her mom looked at him. "Is that why they have such a hard time keeping a General Manager?" she asked, softly.

"I think so. And any other staff for that matter."

"Because of a ghost." Her mom's eyes suddenly sparkled. "Remind me to thank her. Or him."

"I will." Her dad laughed.

Tabby stood up. "I think I saw the ghost."

Her parents turned to look at her.

"Yeah." She gave a slight shiver. "When you two were in the ballroom. Of course I didn't know that's what it was."

"Tabby, don't make up stories." Her mom turned to hang up her sweater in the closet.

"I'm not! I saw something moving along behind you while you were dancing."

Tabby's mom frowned and looked at her dad. "Dancing."

"Yeah, a faint white figure in the mirror, floating along after you. It was—spooky." Tabby bit her lip. "I don't think that Jana saw it, though."

Tabby's dad slid his arm around her mom and both of them frowned at Tabby. "You're sure?"

Tabby straightened indignantly. "Of course I'm sure!" She took a deep, unsteady breath. "I wouldn't make something like that up."

"No. You wouldn't," he agreed. He reached out and fluffed her hair. "And I guess if anyone would know, it would be you."

Tabby nodded.

"Next time, though, tell us," her mother said, grinning and giving her a poke in the side. "So we can see them, too."

Tabby shook her head. Somehow, she got the feeling that her parents weren't taking this very seriously.

* * *

Tabby was perched on one of the windowsills in the ballroom, watching several staff members unwrap the chandeliers and furnishings, decorate the large room and discuss the latest scare by the hotel's resident ghost.

Apparently, it had appeared at a recital that had been held in the ballroom the evening before and had brought the entertainment to an abrupt halt as musicians and guests alike had fled screaming.

Tabby was fascinated. She had spent most of this first morning prowling the corridors of the hotel, getting the layout straight in her head, but now she sat with crossed ankles, trying to keep her balance on her narrow seat.

"Well, I don't know why I keep on working here, that's all I can say!" A round, white-haired woman in a snowy apron was directing the placement of several pots of plants and flowers.

"C'mon, April, you know we couldn't get along without you!" one of the young men working with her walked past with a large planter on a dolly.

"Pooh. You'd do fine, Harry," April said.

"And you probably know more about the ghost than anyone," Harry went on. "What do *you* have to be frightened of?"

"Well, I'm just getting tired of the whole thing," she said.

"Here's where I hit you back with your favourite word." He grinned. "Pooh."

April laughed.

"Do you really know all about the ghost?" Tabby said, sliding to her feet.

April spun around, one hand on her heart. "Goodness, child, you frightened me! Where did you pop up from?"

"I've been sitting over there." Tabby pointed. "Just watching you set up."

"Ah." April put her head on one side and looked at Tabby with snapping dark eyes. "You must be the new manager's daughter."

"I'm Tabby Pillay. Dad calls me Tabs and Mom calls me her Tabby Cat."

"Well, it is nice to meet you, Tabby Pillay, aka Tabs, aka Tabby Cat," April said, offering her hand. "I'm April. Aka Hotel Events. Welcome to the Overlook Hotel." She smiled at Tabby. "And I think you can be our little Kitten!"

"Umm—okay." Tabby took the proffered hand. It felt soft and puffy, like its owner. She grinned. "Hello, April."

April looked past Tabby. "Oh, George, I want that over there." She pointed as another young man entered the room with a large and ornate bouquet of flowers. Then she turned back. "So what do you want to know about the ghost?"

"Everything." Tabby leaned closer and lowered her voice to a whisper. "I think I saw it!"

April raised her eyebrows. "You saw it? Were you at the recital?"

Tabby shook her head. "No. We were getting settled in our rooms and missed that. But earlier in the day, yeah, I think I saw it." Tabby pointed. "Right there, when we were taking the tour."

April followed the pointing finger. "When you were taking the tour?" She frowned. "So—during the day?"

Tabby wrinkled her forehead, thinking. "Yeah. It would have been about 2:00 or so yesterday afternoon."

"Really?"

Tabby nodded. "Yeah."

"Well." April walked over to one of the large planters and perched on the edge. "Come over and talk to me, Kitten, while I take a breather."

"What do you need a breather for? We're the ones doing all the work!" George asked as he headed back toward the door.

"Keep that up and, grandson or no grandson, you'll find another job!"

George laughed.

April looked back at Tabby and shook her head. "That's what I get for hiring relatives!" She grinned. "Now, tell me what you saw."

"Well, my parents were dancing." Tabby sat, cross-legged at April's feet.

"Dancing?"

"Yeah." Tabby nodded. "They used to do it a lot. Before my dad got sick."

April seemed to digest that for a moment. Then, "But did they have—music?"

Tabby shrugged. "Well, not really. Just my dad humming. He's got a really nice voice, though. He always sings to me at night after we read stories."

April was silent for a moment. Then she nodded. "That would explain it, then." She looked at Tabby. "Up until now, our ghost has only been spotted when music is playing. Live music."

Tabby nodded. "At the other hotels I've lived in, we usually had live orchestras playing at night and the occasional pianist or soloist during the day."

"Yes," April said. "That is usually what happens here."

"So—something like that would supposedly attract the ghost?"

"Yes."

"Like my dad singing."

April nodded thoughtfully. "Must be," she said.

"So, anyway, tell me about this ghost." Tabby inched closer.

"Well, no one knows very much about it. We know that it first appeared just before this hotel opened and that it is a tall child or a small adult, but that is about all. No one has ever been able to see its face."

Tabby stared. "Why not? Doesn't it have one?"

April smiled. "Oh, I'm sure it does. But it is veiled, you see. Draped from head to foot in a long cloth."

"Weird." Tabby frowned. "A long cloth. A long, *white* cloth?"

"Yes."

Tabby glanced toward the windows. "Has it ever been seen out on the roof?"

April stared at her. "On the roof?"

"Yeah. When we got here yesterday, I saw someone dressed in something long and white standing out on the roof."

April frowned and shook her head. "I've never heard of anything like that. Tell me exactly what you saw."

Tabby scratched her nose and scrunched up her eyes thoughtfully. "My parents and I had just driven up and Dad was getting the suitcases out of the back. I looked up and saw someone standing on the roof. Just—standing there. Then, whoever it was turned toward us and I got the weirdest feeling. Sorta shivery and strange. Like all of my hair had just stood on end."

April pursed her lips. "That does sound like our ghost. But was there any music?"

Tabby frowned. "Not that I can remember," she said finally.

11

"That is strange."

"Well, it sure scared me!" Tabby looked at April and made a face.

April smiled. "Yes. It is quite good at that. It always causes quite a stir whenever and wherever it appears."

"I can guess," Tabby said.

"But still, people insist on holding their important functions here." April smiled. "This is the nicest hotel in these parts, and I can hardly blame them for wanting the best, but even so—"

"Maybe they hope it won't show." Tabby frowned thoughtfully. "Or maybe they *want* to be scared."

April shrugged. "Well, some people are certainly fascinated by ghosts and ghost stories," she agreed.

Tabby nodded. "In Banff, my friends and I spent hours looking for the hotel's ghosts."

April's eyes twinkled. "And did you ever meet up with them?"

"No," Tabby said sadly. "But we had great times looking!" She sighed. "You know, it's lots more fun looking for ghosts when you have someone with you. When you're by yourself, it's—spooky."

April laughed.

"So does anyone know who your ghost is?" Tabby asked. "Or who it—was?"

"Mr. Withers might know more than I do," April said. "He built this hotel and has owned it for over sixty years and he might have found out—I don't know—something?"

Tabby frowned and rolled her eyes as she thought about the strange man her family had met the day before. "I'm not sure I'd ever want to talk to *him*," she said.

April laughed. "Well, he is a bit difficult to get to know," she said. "But he's actually quite nice. In a scary sort of way."

"Great!" Tabby said sarcastically, making a face. "Just the sort of person *I* want to be friends with."

Just then, Tabby's mother appeared in the door. "Oh, Tabby Cat, there you are!" she said. "I've been looking for you. Time for lunch." She hurried away.

Tabby scrambled to her feet. "Thanks for talking to me, April," she said.

April laughed again and stood up. "It's been a pleasure, Kitten," she said. "But, I suppose I should get back to work—"

"How can you get back to something you've never started?" George demanded as he came through the door with another bouquet of flowers.

"George, I'm going to take the switch to you!" April said.

George laughed.

"Come and talk to me again, Tabby!" April called as Tabby headed for the door.

"I will!" Tabby waved.

* * *

Tabby took a big bite of her sandwich and chewed for a moment. "It comes out when there's music playing," she told her parents.

"Ugh!" her mom said. "Tabs, swallow first!"

"Sorry!" Tabby mumbled. She reached for her glass of milk and took a big swig.

Her father frowned. "When there's music, you say."

"But when you saw it, there wasn't any music," her mom said.

Tabby nodded toward her father. "Well, Dad was singing."

Her mother smiled at her dad. "He was, wasn't he?" She clasped his hand.

"If you call that singing." Her dad laughed.

"Could we get back to my story?"

"Sorry honey," her mom said. "We tend to get a bit sidetracked."

Tabby knew that her mom had been terrified that her dad would die. She really didn't blame her parents for making eyes at each other every chance they got, but it got a bit tiring for the third person in the room.

"So what do you think?" she asked.

Her dad turned to look at her. "About what?"

Tabby rolled her eyes. "About the ghost coming out when you were singing."

"All I can say is that it doesn't have much of a taste for music!" Her dad grinned.

"David! How can you say such a thing?" her mom said.

He laughed and got to his feet. "Well, I'd better get back to it."

"David!" Tabby's mom protested. "You've only been here for fifteen minutes!"

He sighed. "I'd love to stay longer, but I've got a lot to learn as quickly as possible."

Her mom sighed and nodded. "I know."

He kissed her. "I'll be back soon, hon."

"Not soon enough," her mom grumbled.

"Bye, honey," her dad gave Tabby a kiss on the top of her head. "Be good."

Tabby straightened. "I'm always good!"

"That you are," he said. "I'm off!"

Her mom got up and started to clear the table. "What have you got planned for this afternoon, honey?"

"Oh I just thought I'd explore. A bit more."

"You're a poet and don't know it," her mom said, kissing the tip of her nose.

Tabby shook her head. Parents were so weird.

Her mom loaded some dishes into the dishwasher and came back to the table. "Old hotels are great fun to explore, aren't they? Put your dishes into the washer, honey."

"Well, haunted ones are." Tabby got to her feet and found a spot to put her plate and cup.

"Just don't get your hopes up too high. You know how unpredictable ghosts are. You might never see it again."

Tabby rinsed her hands in the sink. "Yeah. Well, I didn't give up at Banff!"

"You're right, there." Her mom grinned. "You practically haunted those halls yourself."

Tabby smiled. It had been such fun with her friends, Cassie and Laurie, exploring seldom-used corridors, cameras ready, just in case one of the hotel spirits decided to pay them a visit. They never saw anything remotely ghostly, but they had enjoyed trying. "I wish Cassie and Laurie were here," she said softly.

"Oh, honey. " Her mom gave her a hug. "You'll make other friends."

Tabby looked up at her mom. "Hey, since all three of us are on summer break, maybe I could invite them to come here for a few days!" she said, hopefully.

Her mom laughed. "They would certainly be welcome." She kissed the top of her daughter's head. "My word, Tabby Cat, you're getting so tall!"

"You'd better stop feeding me, Mom."

Her mom laughed again. "Well, that is one solution," she said. She stepped back. "Have a fun afternoon, honey," she said. "Get lots of exploring done and enjoy your summer."

"Thanks, Mom!" Tabby moved out into the hall. "I'll try," she said under her breath.

# Chapter 3: Where Tabby has a Closer-Than-Expected Encounter. In Higher-Than-Expected Places.

Tabby was exploring the hotel attics.

She was picking her way carefully through a narrow corridor formed by sheet-shrouded furniture when, brushing against something, she was suddenly enveloped in a cascade of dust.

She sneezed violently. "Man! It's dusty up here," she said to herself, her voice sounding loud in the stillness.

For a moment, she questioned the restless urge that had brought her up here. But in the three weeks since they had arrived, she had explored every other part of the hotel and the attics were all that was left.

She shrugged and started forward once more, but bumped into something, and then, trying to recover, banged her shin painfully against whatever stood opposite. Disgusted, she hopped on one foot while she tried to see how badly she had been wounded.

Finally, she dropped her foot back to the floor and aimed a kick at the offender. This time, she stubbed her toe painfully.

The cloth cover slipped and Tabby was looking at a large ladies' make-up table with gracefully carved legs. A great round mirror, obviously meant to be part of the piece, stood behind it.

She stopped and ran a finger across the beautiful, deep-grained wood. "Wow! Pretty fancy," she said.

Suddenly, she caught movement in the mirror and leaned over the table to look into it closely.

She saw nothing. Had she imagined it? The flash of white?

She shook her head and threw the cover back up over the table and mirror, then continued exploring. Finally, she had worked her way to the far end of the great room. A small, dusty window looked out over the roof and she climbed the two steps leading to it.

She pressed her face against the sun-warmed glass and peered through. Dimly, she could make out the roof below her.

She turned from the window and looked back across the attic at the weird forest of spooky, white cloth-covered objects which rose up before her.

Suddenly, part way down the row, one of the cloths moved and Tabby's eyes darted toward it as it slid, silently, to the ground, uncovering the dressing table she had been examining seconds before.

She frowned. Then, "I must not have put it back properly," she said loudly. She walked over to the cloth and picked it up.

Suddenly in the mirror behind the dresser, she caught a glimpse of—a figure. Someone was looking at her just over her left shoulder.

Smothering a shriek of alarm, Tabby spun around.

Nothing.

She turned slowly back to the mirror, clutching the cloth against herself protectively. Then she shrank back against the sheet-shrouded piece of furniture behind her and stared.

The figure—white-draped and shapeless—was still there, watching her. The features were hidden and Tabby could just make out the shadow of dark eyes.

Then, as suddenly as it had appeared, it vanished and only Tabby's somewhat pale face showed in the dark glass.

For a second, Tabby remained frozen, peering wide-eyed into the glass, her heart hammering in her chest.

Finally, she turned and, weaving her way wildly along the narrow aisle, flew back to the stairway.

She had had more than enough of exploring attics.

At the top of the stairs, she stopped and glanced one last time behind her. For a moment, to her excited imagination, the various pieces of shrouded furniture seemed be floating and bobbing before her.

Then the door below her burst open, smacking against the inside wall.

Tabby stifled a shriek and leaned back against the wall, one hand pressed against her heart as her father's voice came clearly up the stairs.

"There should be room up here, Paul. And while we're at it, we might as well see what else we can find."

"Dad!" Tabby shouted.

Her father appeared at the bottom of the stairs and looked up. "Tabs! What are you doing here?"

"Dad, I'm so glad to see you! You'll never believe what I just—"

Her father reached back through the open door. A heavy brass headboard appeared. Then another man.

For a moment, Tabby stared at the two of them.

"Tabs?" He dad had stopped and was staring up at her. "Are you okay? What are you doing up here?"

Tabby jumped. "Oh. Well—I'm just—exploring," she finally managed, shakily.

"Oh. Good." Her dad glanced at the man behind him. "Paul and I are on the prowl to find antiques for the auction."

"Auction?"

"Remind me later to tell you about it."

"Umm. Okay. Uh—Dad?"

He looked up again. "What is it Tabs?" He and Paul started up the stairs toward her carrying the heavy, brass fixture.

"I—I—" Tabby couldn't get any further.

Her dad stopped a couple of steps below her and frowned. "You're looking pale, hon. Are you feeling all right?"

"Umm—yeah, I guess so. Only—"

She had to move to one side as her dad and the other man finished wrestling the heavy headboard up the stairs.

"What, Tabs?" her dad asked as he and Paul passed her.

Tabby glanced back along the narrow aisle and shivered. "Umm—nothing," she mumbled. "I'll talk to you about it later."

Her dad frowned at her. "Okay, Tabs. Are you sure you're feeling all right?"

Tabby hesitated. Then, "Umm—yeah, I'm sure," she said. She slowly turned and, clinging to the railing, made her way shakily down to the fourth floor.

In the weeks since she and her parents had arrived, this floor had been the most fun. Mostly because it had no guest rooms. It consisted of one large hallway that ran completely around the top of the hotel; fitted with large windows on either side. The interior windows looked inward over the great ballroom four storeys below. The exterior windows looked far out over the rolling farmland, providing the view that gave the Overlook its name.

Even though the view was incredible, guests seldom came up here. The elevators didn't reach this floor, so access was by stairway only. Most of them didn't even know it existed and those that did were reluctant to make the trip up the narrow, steep stairs. And that was just fine with Tabby. It was the closest she would ever get to having a secret hang-out and she spent a lot of time spying—unseen—down on the ballroom activities, or gazing out across the countryside.

Now, still trying to calm herself, she leaned her hot forehead against one of the cool inner windows and peered out into the ballroom. The place was deserted, lit only by the setting sun as it attempted to pour through the thick drapes on the west windows.

Obviously the Breakfast League of Ladies, with their great, swishing dresses, flapping hands and shrill voices, who had been in possession of the hall the entire morning, had been shooed away. As had their endless tea and cakes and chatter.

Also obviously, no one was expecting to use the ballroom that night; or set-up would have been well underway.

Tabby started to turn away when something moved down below. She pressed her face back to the window.

Someone, dressed in white, was walking across the ballroom floor.

Tabby peered at them intently. No, someone was *floating* across the ballroom floor. Abruptly the figure turned, then lifted gracefully off the ground.

"Ooh!" Tabby moaned, before she clamped her hands tightly over her mouth.

In an instant, the figure was directly outside of Tabby's window, peering in at her.

19

Tabby gasped, then dropped to the floor.

"What's the matter, Tabs?"

Tabby squeaked again and lifted her head.

Her father and the man who had been helping him were looking at her. "Are you okay?" her dad asked.

Tabby got shakily to her feet and, moving quickly over to her father, reached for his hand. Only then did she glance at the now-empty window. "There was—there was—was—" She looked back at the two men.

Both were staring at her, puzzled.

Tabby tried again. "I—saw—" She shook her head and frowned, feeling close to tears. Standing here with the two very real men staring at her, what she had seen suddenly seemed too fantastic. "I'm not sure what I saw," she managed finally in a small voice.

Her dad frowned and glanced around, finally stepping over to the window, pulling his daughter along with him as she refused to give up her grip on his hand. "Was there something down there?" he asked.

"Sort of." Tabby glanced toward the window, then quickly away.

Her father's frown deepened. "Tabs, you're scaring me!" he said, a little more sharply. "What happened?"

Tabby's lips quivered and she pressed them together. She looked at her dad. "Dad, I hate it here!" she whispered. "Can we go home now?"

She dropped his hand and hurried off down the hall toward the stairway.

* * *

A short time later, Tabby's dad was staring at her intently across the dinner table. "Want to tell me about it, Tabs?"

"Oh, Dad, you're going to think I'm making things up again."

"Tabs, I saw your face up there. I know you aren't making anything up!"

Tabby sighed. Finally, she looked at her Dad. "I saw the ghost again. Twice."

Her dad stared at her. "Twice?"

"Yeah. In the attic and then through the ballroom window."

"Is that why you were looking so—piqued—when we saw you up there."

Tabby nodded.

"So where in the attic? And what did you see?"

She sighed. "In a mirror. At first I thought someone was standing behind me and I turned around to see who it was. But there was no one there. Then when I turned back to the mirror, the—the figure was still there. Just staring at me." She frowned. "It was really creepy, Dad."

"Can you describe the person?"

Tabby frowned. "Not really. It was covered in some sort of cloth."

Her dad sat back in his chair and rubbed a hand over his face. Then he looked at her once more. "I'm sure you are seeing the hotel ghost. But what I can't figure out is why it seems to have changed its usual pattern."

"Yeah." Tabby nodded. "Everyone says it only comes out when music is playing. Well there certainly wasn't any music in the attic! Or the ballroom!" She looked at her father. "And why does it keep appearing to me?"

He shook his head. "I simply don't know, Tabs."

"Well I hate it!" Tabby said. "And I want to go home!"

The door opened just as she spoke.

"What's this you're saying?" Tabby's mom backed through the door, carrying a large, silver tray.

Tabby looked over at her mom and bit her lip.

"Our girl has had a bit of a scare today," her dad said.

"A bit of a scare?!" Tabby said, her voice rising. She turned to her mom. "I saw the ghost! Twice! It was right in my face!"

Her mother stared at her. "Really?"

"Yeah. In the attics and in the ballroom."

Her mom looked at her dad. "Did you see it too?"

"No such luck," her dad said.

21

"Luck!" Tabby screeched, getting to her feet. "You think being scared half to death is luck?"

"Calm down, honey," her dad said, standing and sliding his arm around her shoulders. "In all of the years that the ghost has been appearing here, there have been no reports of it hurting anyone."

Tabby shrugged him off and stepped away. "Yeah, well it only appeared at *dances* before this," she pointed out. "If it's changing how it does things, who knows what else it may change!"

Her parents stared at her. "She does have a point," her mom said at last.

Her father sighed. "I'm sorry about that and I'm as confused and upset as you are." He looked at both of them and folded his arms. "But we can't let this scare us off. We can't simply leave."

Tabby sat back in her chair and folded her arms. For a moment, father and daughter looked very much alike. "Well, don't say I didn't warn you," she said.

"Look, let's not discuss it now," her mom said. "Let's have a nice meal and then we can talk about it afterwards."

She moved to the table and set the heavy tray down. "Sorry, but I ordered from the dining room tonight. I got caught up in my computer and lost track of the time."

Tabby's mom was deep into family history research. Sometimes, Tabby suspected that she preferred people long dead to those who were still living.

Tabby rolled her eyes and sighed. Maybe it would be better if she didn't think about dead people right now.

She looked at the dishes on the tray. Prime rib. Garlic mashed potatoes. Rich gravy. Steaming vegetables. She sighed again.

Usually, she rather liked it when her mom ordered take-out. She just didn't think she could appreciate food right now.

"No need to apologize," her dad was saying as he smiled at her mom. "This looks absolutely delicious!"

Her mom grinned. "Well, I told myself that you really need to sample the dishes from the dining room."

Tabby's dad nodded, his smiled growing wider. "Good excuse."

She flushed and returned his smile, then grabbed serving spoons and carving tools from the counter. "Let's eat. I'm starved!"

For the next half-hour, the three of them concentrated on serving and eating and her parents kept the conversation firmly on inconsequential things.

Tabby was surprised to discover that she was hungry. She shoved a bite from her third piece of prime rib into her mouth and started to chew.

"How is the food?" her mom asked, pulling the bowl of mashed potatoes toward her and taking a second helping.

Tabby's dad looked at his nearly-empty plate, then at the depleted serving dishes. "I'd say it was pretty popular."

Tabby's mom smiled. "I have to come to the same conclusion." She looked at Tabby. "What do you say, dear?"

Tabby nodded. "S'good," she said around her mouthful of tender meat.

Her mom's eyes twinkled. "I'm glad."

A short while later, Tabby lay down her fork and knife and heaved a sigh of pure satisfaction. "I really was hungry."

"Yes, you were." Her dad grinned.

"So are we ready to talk about what happened today?" her mom asked.

Tabby shrugged.

Her dad looked at her mom. "Paul and I were taking stuff up to the attics and we found Tabby there looking like she'd seen a—well, you know."

Her mom nodded.

"Then, when we came back to the fourth floor, there was Tabs again, only this time she was lying on the floor!"

"Tabby!" her mom said. "What were you doing on the floor?"

Tabby sighed. "When I was in the attic, I saw the ghost in an old mirror. And then when I went to the fourth floor, I saw it again when I was looking out into the ballroom."

"But how—?"

"It floated up from the floor and was—staring at me through the window," Tabby said.

Her mom frowned sharply "Ooh! I don't blame you for being freaked. That would have freaked *me!*"

"Yeah, well, once would have been bad enough. But after the second time, I—" her voice trailed away.

Her dad put a hand on her arm and gave it a squeeze. "I don't blame you for being frightened. Heck, *I'd* have been frightened!"

Her mom shook her head. "Hmm. It had to have been hovering—like—forty feet above the ballroom floor."

Tabby nodded.

"So, what we need to ask ourselves is why has the ghost suddenly started appearing all over the hotel?" her dad asked, "and notably when there is no music playing."

Tabby and her mom both looked at him and Tabby shrugged. "I don't know."

"Well, let's try to sort this out logically. What is different around the hotel?"

"Well, *we're* here," her mom said finally. "That's different." Her dad nodded.

"And, more importantly," she added, "Tabby is here."

"And it's Tabby who keeps seeing the ghost," her dad said, thoughtfully. "Therefore, we must assume that the ghost is drawn to Tabby! There must be something she wants from her. Or something she needs to tell her."

Tabby stared at her parents, then sighed. "Oh, great." She dropped her head onto folded arms.

* * *

That evening, Tabby was on the front desk, feeling very official as she covered briefly for the Jana, the assistant manager.

"Yes? Can I help you?" she asked, smiling brilliantly as a woman dropped a loaded briefcase on the counter.

The woman stared at her. "Aren't you a bit young to be handling the front desk?"

Tabby's smile dimmed somewhat. "I've been doing it since I could read," she explained patiently.

"Oh." The woman unzipped a pocket of her briefcase and pulled out some sheets of paper. "Well, my name's Bennett. I'm here to check in."

Tabby handled the transaction with the ease of familiarity. She handed the woman's credit card back, along with her receipts and assigned room card. "I do hope you enjoy your stay with us, Ms. Bennett" she said.

"Not likely," Ms. Bennett said, stuffing her receipts into her overloaded briefcase. "I'm here to see a ghost. And from my experience, when an official appears, spirits disappear!"

"Well, I hope you won't be dis—" Tabby's voice trailed off as she stared past the woman.

Standing just inside the doorway of the ballroom was a figure in white.

 Chapter 4: Where Tabby Draws Desk Duty and Ghost Hunters Prove— Annoying.

Tabby felt the hair rise on the back of her neck and her eyes grow huge. Her heart started to hammer painfully in her chest and she had to remind herself to breathe. She immediately shrank down behind the counter until only her eyes and the top of her head poked above it.

Ms. Bennett glanced at her, frowning, then spun around. "Oh!" she said. "Is it—is it—?"

"It's the ghost," Tabby managed barely, her voice coming out in a squeak.

For a moment, Ms. Bennett braced herself against the counter. Then she scrambled frantically in her overstuffed case.

The figure in white remained standing where it was, turned in their direction. It seemed to be about Tabby's height, and was swathed in a long, filmy cloth, which covered its head completely and hung down to the floor.

Tabby could just make out a pair of dark eyes through the cloth.

Ms. Bennett emerged finally, triumphantly, with a camera. "Oh, this is amazing!" she said. Just as her camera clicked, the ghost disappeared.

Ms. Bennett sank to the floor.

Tabby crawled quickly over the counter and dropped to her feet beside the woman. "Are you all right?" she asked.

Ms. Bennett was shaking her head. "Never—" she was saying.

Tabby squatted down. "Ms. Bennett? Are you all right?" she said slowly.

The woman finally looked at her. "I've been waiting so long," she whispered. Then she burst into tears.

* * *

Mr. Withers leaned over the front desk. "Tell me again!" he said, the words coming as more of a command than a request.

Tabby stared at the small man. She knew he was in his late eighties, and that she was nearly the same height, but that didn't seem to make him less powerful or threatening.

"Umm—I was standing in for Jana," she stammered.

"Jana?"

"Yes." Tabby nodded toward the red-headed girl at the opposite end of the counter, currently helping a customer. "She had to—had to—go—"

"Yes. I understand that," Mr. Withers said, waving one hand dismissively. "Tell me what happened."

"Well, Ms. Bennett came in and I processed her check-in."

"Go on."

"And then, just as she was putting her papers away, the ghost appeared."

"There." He pointed.

"Yeah," Tabby nodded, shivering. "Right in the doorway to the ballroom."

"And did—what?"

Tabby frowned. "Who? Ms. Bennett?"

"The ghost, you silly girl!" Mr. Withers barked.

Tabby jumped and blinked. What was it about this man that scared her so much? She swallowed. "Well, the ghost did nothing. Just looked at us."

"You could see its face?"

"Well, no. But the cloth was fairly filmy and I could sort of see its eyes through it."

Mr. Withers slid his hands over his head. "Could you describe it?"

Tabby frowned, then shook her head. "No."

He let his breath out in a 'whoosh' of sound, then leaned on the counter and rubbed his face.

"Mr. Withers?"

"What is it?" he said, wearily, without looking at her.

"Can I go now?"

27

"Yes."

Tabby ran for the elevator.

* * *

"You there! Little girl with the braid!"

Tabby turned around.

Ms. Bennett was hurrying toward her across the yard as fast as a pair of spiked heels and a tight skirt would allow. She stopped beside Tabby and pressed one hand on her side. "I'm not used to running," she gasped.

Tabby frowned. How could someone who claimed to be a ghost chaser, be so obviously out of shape. And dress so inappropriately. Maybe the term 'ghost chaser' was just that—a term.

"What did you need, Ms. Bennett?" Tabby asked politely.

"Just a minute, my dear," Ms. Bennett panted. "Let me catch my breath!"

Tabby tried to control her impatience as the woman gasped and coughed.

Finally, she straightened. "Okay, I'm ready," she announced.

For what? Tabby thought. A heart attack? Aloud she said, "Okay."

"So what can you tell me about the ghost we saw last night?" Ms. Bennett asked.

Tabby frowned. "Not much, I'm afraid. She started appearing here just before the hotel opened in 1951. And she used to show up only when there was music. Now she seems to show up at any time."

Ms. Bennett nodded. "Well, I've been talking to the staff. And I've discovered that her appearances became more frequent in the past few weeks. Seemingly after you and your family arrived."

Tabby frowned and was silent for a moment. "Yeah," she said finally. "We sort of figured that out, too."

Ms. Bennett looked at her closely. "Do you have some sort of connection with this ghost?"

Tabby stared at her, frowning. "I don't know," she said slowly.

"But you must! According to everyone here, you are the person who keeps seeing her!"

Tabby scuffed her grubby runner in the gravel of the drive and shrugged.

Ms. Bennett looked down at her own pointed, red shoes. Then she reached into her bag and pulled out a pad and pen. "Well, can you at least tell me about the times you have seen this ghost?"

Tabby nodded unhappily. For some reason, she didn't want to tell this woman about her private brushes with the ghost. She described her experiences in as few words as possible.

"Well, that is fascinating!" Ms. Bennett said, tapping the pad with her pen. "I think it's pretty obvious that she is seeking you out."

"Well, we don't know that!" Tabby said defensively. "She may appear to lots of people! They just aren't talking about it."

Ms. Bennett tipped her head to one side and studied Tabby curiously. "Do you honestly think that someone who sees a ghost wouldn't immediately tell everyone they meet?' she asked softly.

"I—guess so." Tabby said uncertainly. She frowned and went on, "But I also think that if the ghost is following me, it's because it wants to! For some reason of its own. And if it wanted everyone to know about it, it would follow them!" She looked at Ms. Bennett. "And I know just how it feels. I'd hate having people following me!"

She was surprised to see Ms. Bennett's eyes twinkle suddenly. "Well said, dear," she said, giving Tabby a wink. "And I agree with you." She stuffed her pad back into her bag. "Thank you. And you don't have to worry. I won't bother you anymore!" She turned and picked her way back across the gravel to the lawn and from there to the front door.

Once inside, she stopped. Turning, she placed her elbows on the tall sill and peered through the glass at Tabby, obviously there to stay.

Tabby sighed. Great, she though sarcastically. Ms. Bennett may not be 'bothering' Tabby up close. But it looked as though she wasn't about to leave, either.

Now Tabby appeared to have two people following her around—one dead and one living.

* * *

For the next few days, every time Tabby set foot outside of her family's apartment, she could hear the tapping of pointed, high-heeled shoes, either staccato on the tiles or slightly muffled by the carpets, but always just a few steps behind her.

When she looked around, it was to catch glimpses of Ms. Bennett dodging in her best 'ghost sleuth' manner, around corners or behind furniture. It was annoying, but in a strangely comical way.

On the third evening of the woman's stay, Tabby was sitting in what was fast becoming her favourite chair—a huge old over-stuffed horsehair-covered monstrosity that sat in the dimmest corner of the front lobby.

Hearing the skittering of feet on tile, Tabby looked up from the book she was reading and caught a glimpse of a bright red suit dodging behind the grand piano.

She rolled her eyes.

Ms. Bennett, obviously.

Tabby snapped her book closed, pulled herself from the chair and started deliberately toward the woman's hiding place.

When she was halfway across the room, Ms. Bennett suddenly squeaked and sprang to her feet. Teetering precariously, and clutching her precious camera, the woman fled up the stairs toward the second floor.

Tabby chuckled and reversed her direction, moving, instead toward the ballroom.

"Tabs! Where are you going?"

Tabby glanced over at the front desk. Her father had just emerged from the office behind the counter and was looking at her over his reading glasses.

"Just—checking out the ballroom," Tabby said. "It's been—days since I last saw the ghost. I wanted to make sure she was all right."

Her father gave a little snort of laughter. "Well, they're just finishing up with the Tatum tea," he said. "Don't get in anyone's way!"

"Dad!" Tabby was disgusted. "How many teas have I helped put up and take down?"

Her dad grinned. "Lots?"

"Right." Tabby turned and walked through the doors.

The tables had been stacked on long, wheeled carts and the crew was just finishing up with the chairs.

A young man grabbed the handle of the first of the carts and started towing it toward the storage rooms. Another fell in behind him.

"Wagons, ho!" someone shouted.

Everyone laughed and then, suddenly, they stopped.

Tabby looked at them.

All eyes were staring at her.

She froze and felt her face grow hot. Then she frowned as she realized they weren't looking at her. Instead, they were looking at something just behind her.

Tabby spun around.

There was the figure in white, mere feet away.

The little bubble of determination that had stiffened her spine and brought her bravely into the ballroom disappeared as though it had never been. She gasped and stepped back.

It seemed to be the signal for everyone else in the room to scream loudly and find somewhere else to be.

Vaguely, Tabby heard voices shrieking and calling and the sound of pounding feet. Not taking her eyes from the ghostly shape, she began to back slowly away, finally stopping as she bumped into something solid. She reached behind herself with a cold and tentative hand and encountered a stack of tables.

The ghost lifted one hand, palm up, almost pleadingly.

Tabby stared at it.

Suddenly, it lifted the other hand and began to move slowly toward her.

31

Tabby felt her eyes grow huge. She began to look frantically around for somewhere—anywhere—to hide.

Just as she turned back toward the ghost, she was blinded by a bright flash.

She blinked. When she opened her eyes again, the ghost was gone.

Ms. Bennett was standing in the ballroom doorway. She lowered her camera. "I knew it!" she said. "I knew that if I stuck close to you, I'd get another shot!"

* * *

Tabby sat down at the breakfast table the next morning and put her head into her hands.

Her mother set a bowl of steaming oatmeal in front of her and pushed the cream and sugar closer. Then she sat down opposite and resumed eating.

Tabby picked up the cream. "So what was all the shouting about?" she asked.

Her mother looked at her.

"Last night. Someone was shouting."

"I'm sorry, dear, I hadn't realized you would have been disturbed." Her mother put her spoon down.

She looked tired. She sighed and ran her fingers through the long, blonde hair so much like Tabby's and took a deep breath. "That woman? The ghost hunter person?"

Tabby stopped pouring and looked at her. "Yeah?"

"Well she pitched over the bannister onto the lobby floor in the middle of the night."

Tabby blinked and set the cream pitcher down carefully. "What?"

"That woman? You know, the one who wears the impossible heels."

"The one who's been following me every waking moment for the past three days?" Tabby said. "Yeah, I know her."

"Well sometime after 2:00 this morning, she pitched over the second floor bannister onto the lobby floor."

"Is she—is she—d-d—"

"She's got a badly broken wrist. She also bumped her head quite hard and they're pretty sure she has a concussion. She has some other bruises too, and they think she might have sprained an ankle, but other than her wrist, most of her injuries should be all right in a few days."

"How did it happen?" Tabby asked.

Her mom shrugged. "No one knows. Paul was on the front desk and he said that everything was pretty quiet. Then he heard the sound of voices and the next thing he knew, that woman was laying on the floor."

"Voices?" Tabby said. "He heard voices?"

"That's what he said." Her mother yawned.

"What does Ms. Bennett say?" Tabby's breakfast was forgotten.

Her mom shrugged. "I don't think she's saying anything right now except for, 'Ouch, that hurts.' And she's lucky to be able to say that!"

"Voices." Tabby looked at her mother. "Do they think it was—attempted murder?" Her last words were spoken in a whisper.

"No one knows," her mother said, shrugging. "The police have been here since about three, questioning everyone."

"Wow! Things were never this exciting at Banff," Tabby said.

Her mother looked at Tabby, her eyes suddenly filling with tears. "That's the first time you've sounded happy to be here, Tabs," she said.

"Yeah, well—" Tabby grinned. "I guess a ghost and attempted murder would make anything more exciting."

Her mom shook her head and dabbed at her eyes. "Maybe for you." She sighed. "Now you're happy to be here and I'm almost ready to leave!"

The door opened and Tabby's dad walked in. "Got any of that oatmeal for me?" he asked, plopping down into the chair beside Tabby. "I'm starving."

Her mom got up and spooned some into a bowl. "So what's happening?" She set it before him.

He leaned over and nabbed the sugar bowl. "Well, the police have gone over things quite thoroughly." He tipped some sugar onto his oatmeal and set the bowl down. "All of the other guests are pretty well accounted for." He reached for the cream. "And besides, there is no evidence that anyone else was up there with her. They are beginning to suspect that it was merely an unfortunate accident." He looked at Tabby's mom. "You saw the heels she tottered around on."

Tabby's mom nodded. "Definitely a sprained ankle waiting to happen."

Tabby looked at her father. "But Mom said Paul heard voices. *Voices*. Plural."

Tabby's dad looked at her mom. Then shrugged. "Well, the cleaning staff had vacuumed the carpets up there just a short time before the incident and the only footmarks in the thick pile were those belonging to Ms. Bennett." He poured cream. "So, unless the other person—or persons—
have figured out how to move around without touching the carpet—" he stopped. Stared at Tabby and her mom.

"I think our neighbourhood ghost has been doing some midnight skulking," Tabby's mom said.

Her dad nodded. "I think she has been doing more than that."

Chapter 5: Contact. Just That. Contact.

"Where do you want this, April?" Tabby asked. She had gone looking for April and something constructive to do when the police started questioning everyone in the hotel for the second time.

It had already been a long day and it was only half over.

"Over here, Kitten," the elderly woman said, patting the freshly-dusted table top.

Tabby deposited the heavy tray of glasses with a sigh of relief.

April immediately started arranging the glasses in a pyramid while Tabby looked around.

The two of them were in one of the first floor rooms. They were larger than those on the floors above, and many had adjoining hospitality suites - perfect for guests who wanted to host a party.

Floor-to-ceiling windows filled one wall and looked out into the ballroom below. There was even a small balcony, for the guests who wanted to step out during a ball and watch the dancers. At this time, however, the heavy curtains were drawn, blocking out any possible view.

April straightened and surveyed her handiwork. "There. Guaranteed to look pretty."

"And fall down as soon as someone tries to take one," Tabby said over the older woman's shoulder.

"Oh, go on with you!" April laughed. She waved a hand toward the closed drapes. "Tabby, dear, could you please see if the crew has arrived?" she said.

Tabby tried to find the pull for the heavy curtains, but finally gave up and slipped between them.

Someone had turned on one bank of lights at the far end of the ballroom.

Tabby pressed her face against the cool glass and tried to peer down toward them.

Suddenly, another face appeared just inches away. A face swathed in white.

"Oh!" Tabby gasped, instinctively jerking backwards. She got tangled in the curtains and fell over. Squeaking loudly, she finally managed to roll out from underneath.

April put her hands on her hips and stared at her. "Tabby, what are you doing?"

Tabby got shakily to her feet. "The—the—the—" she gasped, pointing.

"What?" April found the cord, pulled it, and the curtains slid back smoothly.

There was no one there.

Tabby stared for a moment and then shook her head. For some stupid reason, she felt close to tears. "Of course," she said. She went back to the window. "I'm getting really tired of this."

April put her arm around Tabby's shoulders. "Don't fret, Kitten," she said. "I'm sure there's a reason it's seeking you out. It'll get around to it."

"Yeah, well, I wish it'd hurry!" Tabby pounded her fists on the glass. "These sudden appearances are going to give me a heart attack!"

April chuckled. "Hardly that, Kitten."

Tabby peered out into the ballroom. "The crew has arrived."

* * *

That evening, Tabby was sitting quietly on a bench just outside the door of the ballroom, listening to the music.

Until a few minutes before, her parents had been sitting there with her, but the music had proved too tempting and they had ducked into the ballroom for a quick waltz.

Tabby sighed. The orchestra was good. In her short eleven years, she had heard enough of them to know. She leaned her head back against the wall and closed her eyes.

Very good.

The music stopped and Tabby could hear someone speaking on the mike.

Two couples came out of the room.

Tabby opened her eyes and watched them walk past.

"She looks just lovely," one of the women was saying.

"Oh, I don't know. I really don't care for her gown," the other woman said. She turned to her companion. "What do you think, Rob?" she demanded.

He looked at her, surprised. "Oh—umm—she's the one wearing the white dress, right?" he stammered.

"Good answer," the other man said.

The four of them laughed and disappeared up the stairway.

Tabby felt a presence beside her and turned, thinking her parents had returned. She felt the blood drain from her face.

A figure about Tabby's size, its face and body hidden beneath a long, white cloth, was sitting on the bench. Tabby could see the stripes of the bench upholstery through it.

"Oh!" Tabby slapped both hands against her mouth and instinctively slid sideways off the bench, landing with a thump on the thick carpet. Then she scrambled awkwardly to her hands and knees and started crawling frantically away.

"*Oh, please don't go!*" the ghost said. There was something desperate in the words. "*Please. I so need to talk to you!*"

Tabby slowed. Then finally stopped and turned her head to look back.

The ghost had remained sitting on the bench. "*Please,*" it said again, holding up a pleading hand.

The voice was a whisper of sound. Faint and hollow as though it came from the bottom of a barrel. But it echoed through the great room and wrapped itself around Tabby until it seemed to be coming from every direction at once.

Tabby scrambled to her feet. "But you're a—you're a— you're the—" Tabby couldn't get the words out.

"*The ghost,*" it said, sadly. "*Yes. I know.*"

Tabby rubbed her eyes, hard, with the heels of her hands. Then she dropped them and looked again.

The ghost was still there.

"*Please talk to me,*" it said again, patting the bench beside it.

Tabby looked at it. "You're not going to—scare me, are you?" she asked.

"*Not intentionally,*" it said.

Tabby could see the faint lines of a mouth curve into a smile beneath the cloth as she slowly approached her seat.

The ghost patted the bench again. "*Please.*"

Tabby perched carefully on the edge, as far from her luminous companion as she could get. She took a deep breath. "Okay," she said nervously. "Talk."

The ghost laughed. "*Well, it's not quite that easy,*" it said. "*You can't just order one into speech and have them comply.*"

"What?" Tabby saw the mouth curve again.

"*What I meant to say was that I must gather my thoughts.*"

"Okay." Tabby waited as the silence stretched.

"Are you sure you know which car is theirs?" It was a man's voice.

Tabby looked up.

A large, happy group of people had come out of the ballroom. They glanced at Tabby and smiled, then continued on.

"Of course," another man in the group said. "I paid the best man a hundred dollars to tell me."

"Oh. Right. Like that's a guarantee."

"You guys have no faith in me!"

"Years of experience have taught us--"

"Never mind. Let's go."

The group disappeared through the front doors.

"Huh," Tabby said after they had gone. "They didn't even seem to see—" She glanced at her companion, but the ghost had vanished.

Tabby got to her feet and looked around. Then she dropped to her knees and looked under the bench.

"*I wish they wouldn't do that!*"

Tabby jumped and hit her head on the solid bottom of the bench. "Ouch!" She sat back on her heels, rubbing the spot.

The ghost was once more sitting where it had been before the interruption.

"Do what?" Tabby asked, still rubbing and feeling just a bit irritated.

The ghost glanced toward the outer door the group of people had used. *"Turn up without warning."* It looked at Tabby. *"It scares me."*

Tabby almost laughed. It seemed funny, somehow, that a ghost could be startled by the living.

"Where did you go?"

"I left. I—don't like crowds."

"So you don't like to be seen by large groups of people?" Tabby asked.

The ghost seemed to shiver. *"That's right,"* it said. *"It makes me feel--exposed."*

"But from the stories I've heard, you've appeared dozens of times in rooms *filled* with people," Tabby said.

The ghost lifted a transparent shoulder. *"I just can't help myself when there is music playing,"* it said. *"I so love music. And dancing too, if I knew how."*

Tabby smiled. "I know what you mean," she said. "My parents are like that."

"Are your parents the couple that was dancing one afternoon?"

"Yes. Dad was humming."

"Oh, they are exquisite!"

"I'm going to pretend I know what that means," Tabby said.

"They dance beautifully!"

"Yeah, I think so, too," Tabby said. She looked at the ghost. "So what did you want to talk to me about?" she asked.

"Well, it's difficult," the ghost said.

"Shoot!" Tabby said.

"Excuse me?"

"Go ahead."

"Oh. Of course. I'm not used to your modern forms of speaking."

"Yeah." Tabby grinned. "Well, there's a lot of times when I don't know what people are saying, either."

"This is going to sound rather strange," the ghost said.

"Sitting here, talking to a ghost doesn't seem strange to you?" Tabby asked. Then she shrugged. "What am I saying—?"

Again, she saw the faint smile. "*I do understand,*" the ghost said. "*It's just that--I've never asked for help before in all of the years I've been here.*" It turned toward Tabby. "*But there's something about you. Something about the way you* feel."

"Really?"

"*Yes. I feel as though you are the one to help me.*"

"Why me?"

"*I don't know.*"

"I'm only eleven," Tabby said. "I can't – you know – drive. Or do much."

"*You will be able to help.*"

"Okay. Shoot."

The ghost smiled again. Then, abruptly, the smile vanished as it looked steadily at Tabby. "*I need you to find me.*"

Tabby felt her eyebrows go up. "Find you?" she asked, confused. "But you're—you're right here."

The ghost sighed softly. Another whisper of sound. "*I mean my body. I need you to find my body.*"

"Your body is lost?"

"*I know this sounds strange to you,*" it said, "*but something prevents me from finding my body--and remembering.*"

Tabby frowned. "So you can't find your way back to your body?"

"*Nor remember who I am or the events surrounding my death.*"

"Bummer," Tabby said.

"*Sorry?*"

"I mean, that's awful."

"*Quite so,*" the ghost said. "*Now, what do you say? Will you help me?*"

Tabby was silent for a moment. "This is kind of weird."

"*I understand that this must sound very strange.*"

Tabby bit her lip and thought for a moment. Finally, "I have school in a few weeks."

"*Oh.*" The ghost seemed to droop.

"Once it starts, I'll only be able to help you in the evenings and on weekends."

It straightened. "*So you* will *help?*"

"I'll try," Tabby said.

"*Oh, you've made me so happy!*"

"So where do we start?" Tabby asked.

"*We-ell,*" the ghost drew the word out. "*I—umm—*"

Tabby looked at it expectantly.

"*As I said, I don't remember much.*"

"My Dad told me that this hotel was built in the fifties," Tabby said. "Have you ever been anywhere else?"

"*No,*" the ghost said. "*I've always been here.*"

Tabby frowned. "So it seems reasonable that this is where you lived."

"*Or at least died.*"

Tabby shivered and scowled. "There is that. But at least it's something to start with."

"*A theory,*" the ghost said. It sighed—an indistinct thread of sound. "*I'm afraid I'm not much help to you,*" it went on. Then the ghost turned toward the doors of the ballroom and nodded. "*Except--I have always felt drawn there.*"

"To the ballroom?"

"*Yes.*"

"Hmmm." Tabby narrowed her eyes.

"*Oh, and one more thing,*" the ghost said.

"What's that?"

"*I would prefer that no one know we have spoken.*"

"Why not?"

"*I don't feel--I can trust other people,*" it said.

"Right. No people. Unless there's music playing. Gotcha."

"*Excuse me?*"

"I meant--okay," Tabby said.

"*Oh. Good.*"

"Let me see what I can find out," Tabby went on.

"*Oh, thank you!*" the ghost said. "*I knew you were the one to help me!*"

Chapter 6: Where the Scariest People Prove—Scary. And Less Than Helpful.

"Well, I just want to find out about the ghost," Tabby told her dad over breakfast the next morning. "What if I told Mr. Withers I'm doing a paper about it? An assignment for school."

Tabby, sometime during a rather sleepless night, had decided that her dad's boss might be her best source of information.

"But school doesn't start for a few more weeks," her dad said. "Besides, I'm not sure if that will make Mr. Withers more— or less—friendly."

Tabby twisted her mouth. "How could he possibly become *less* friendly?"

"Exactly," her mom said.

Her dad shrugged. "Well, I don't see any harm in it. I don't think he'll fire me because you ask him a couple of questions."

Tabby's mom rolled her eyes and grinned at him. "Don't underestimate him."

"So where is his suite?" Tabby asked.

"He lives on the far side of the building from us," her dad said. "The top two floors. He has a private elevator that opens in the car park and again in a small lobby on the main floor before it goes to his suite."

"How do I get to him?"

"Well, I think your best bet would be to wait until he makes a trip into the city. Then you can catch him as he's heading back to his apartment."

Tabby slumped. "How will I know when he goes into town? I'm going to have to take my camping gear and set up in his lobby."

Her dad smiled. "Not quite so drastic, honey. I happen to be going with him to the city on Friday to sign some papers."

"Oooh! Then you can talk to him!"

"Well, I can try—"

* * *

Friday morning, Tabby was sitting on the landing overlooking the main floor lobby, her legs dangling between the bars of the bannister. She leaned her forehead against the uprights and peered down through them.

"*See anything exciting?*"

Startled, Tabby squeaked and caught her breath, pressing one hand to her chest. Then she turned her head to see the ghost standing beside her. It didn't matter that they had met and spoken. The ghost still made Tabby feel—jittery.

She took a deep, calming breath, then finally put her forehead back against the bannister uprights. "Nope," she said, trying to disguise her nervousness. "Nothing exciting. Just— thinking."

The ghost moved closer. "*What are you thinking about?*"

Tabby shivered slightly, then looked at it again. "Actually, I was thinking about Ms. Bennett," she said. "My dad talked to her and she hasn't been able to remember anything that happened just before she fell. And I'm wondering how she ended up going from here to the lobby floor."

The ghost peered over the rail. "*Yes, it is rather curious.*"

Tabby looked at her, suspicion overcoming her anxiety. "Come on," she said. "It had to have been you."

"*What?*" the ghost turned toward her. "*Me?*"

"Well, we know that there was more than one person in this particular spot the night of Ms. Bennett's accident. She was talking to someone. Paul heard *voices*. Plural."

"*Yes.*"

"And that second person didn't leave any footprints in the newly-cleaned carpet."

"*Ah. So you reasoned that it had to have been someone whose feet wouldn't leave any evidence. Me.*"

"Yeah. I'm almost sure that's what I'm saying," Tabby said.

"*Well, I have to disagree with you, because it wasn't me.*"

"Well it must have been another of the thousands of ghosts who haunt this hotel, then," Tabby said sarcastically.

"*Perhaps*," the ghost said.

Tabby spun around to look at it. "What? Are you telling me that there are more ghosts in this hotel?"

"*This is an old hotel. Many, many people have been through its doors.*"

"That's not a 'no'."

The ghost merely shrugged and changed the subject. "*So what have you found out?*"

Tabby frowned at the ghost for a few seconds. Then she sighed and put her forehead back against the uprights. "Nothing. But my dad has gone into town with Mr. Withers and he's going to talk to him and maybe ask him to talk to me."

"*I think I followed that*," the ghost said.

But Tabby wasn't going to be sidetracked for long. "To get back to our more interesting topic, what did you mean about there being other ghosts in the hotel?" She turned to look at her companion.

The ghost was gone.

* * *

That afternoon, Tabby helped her mother with the lunch dishes, then flopped onto her stomach on the couch to read a book and try to ignore the clock ticking on the far wall.

When the phone rang sometime later, she was off the couch and standing beside her mother before the second ring. The older woman picked it up.

Tabby clearly heard her father's voice.

"Tell Tabby we're just pulling into the drive. She can wait for us in the car park!"

Her mother poked a button and dropped her phone, then turned toward her daughter.

But Tabby, clutching a clipboard and pen, was already in the hall and sprinting for the elevator.

She punched the button for the lowest floor and the doors slid silently shut.

"*On your way?*"

Tabby collapsed against the wall of the elevator. "Man, you have to stop scaring me like that!"

"*Sorry,*" the ghost said. "*I keep forgetting that things aren't as obvious to you as they are to me.*"

Tabby glared at it.

"*I can see everyone, even through the walls,*" it went on. "*I keep forgetting that they can't see me until I'm in the same space as they are.*"

Tabby blinked. "You can see through walls."

"*Yes.*"

"But you can't see your body."

"*Something prevents it.*"

"Well, whatever it is, I wish I had some!" Tabby said. "Then you couldn't scare me to death!"

The ghost made a strange sound.

"Are you—you're laughing!" Tabby said.

"*Yes, my friend. The way you speak, it's just so--droll.*"

"That's a good thing, right?"

More laughter.

"I'm going to take that as a 'yes'." Tabby tipped her head to one side. "Are you a boy or a girl?"

The ghost turned and stared at her. "*You don't know?*"

"Well, most of the time I think you're a girl," Tabby said. "But I'm really not sure."

The ghost's shadowy lips parted in a smile. "*That is one thing I do know,*" it said. "*I'm a girl, Tabby.*"

"Oh," Tabby said. "Okay." She was quiet for a moment. Then, "You know, if we're going to keep on meeting, I'm going to have to think of something to call you. Unless you've also remembered your name."

The ghost shook her head.

"Okay, then. How about—Beth?"

"*Beth?*"

"Yeah. That was the name of my cat. Well— Bethboots. But Beth for short."

"*You're naming me after your cat?*"

"I loved that cat. She died." Tabby shrugged. "It—seems appropriate."

"*Oh. Well—I guess that will be fine.*"

"Good. Beth it is."

The doors slid open and the lights of a car shone momentarily into the elevator.

"Oh, they're here. Keep down!" But Tabby was speaking to herself.

Beth had once more vanished.

Tabby jumped from the elevator and followed the car around to the presidential area. She smiled to herself. It was exactly the same as the other parking spots in the underground lot, just nearer to the bank of elevators.

The car pulled into a spot and stopped.

Tabby was standing beside the passenger's door when her father stepped to the pavement. "Here she is, Mr. Withers," he said.

The elderly man looked at Tabby over the top of the car. "So I see. Well, if she needs information, tell her to hurry along."

Not a promising start, but Tabby clutched her clipboard and pen a little tighter and ran after the elderly man.

He inserted the key for his private elevator and gave it a twist and the elevator doors slid smoothly open. "Well?" He glanced at Tabby. "What do you want to know?"

Tabby swallowed and followed him inside. "I'm doing a report for school. About our ghost."

"Ghost! It's all a bunch of hogwash," the old man snorted. "You should write about something real!"

"Well, it's such a popular story and people come from miles around just on the hope—"

"People!" he snorted.

Tabby frowned at him. "Honestly, you need to adjust your attitude, Mr. Withers! People are your bread and butter!"

He looked at her. For the first time, really looked at her. Then he chuckled. "You've got me there, girl. What would you like to know about our famous ghost?"

* * *

46

"Well he still wasn't very friendly," Tabby said a couple of hours later. "But at least he talked to me."

"Did you go to his apartment?"

"Yeah, he took me all the way to his penthouse. It's huge!"

Her dad smiled. "I've been there a few times myself. And I agree."

"So tell us what happened!" her mom begged.

"Well, we got there and his servant took his coat and briefcase and then offered us tea in the *Drawing Room*." Tabby drew the words out.

Her mom put one hand over her mouth and smothered a giggle.

"Then what?" her dad prompted.

"Well, I don't drink tea," Tabby said. "So I had a ginger ale."

"Very good choice," her dad said, his eyes twinkling.

"We sat in this room with a huge fireplace and big, squashy couches and he told me everything he could think of."

"So what could he think of?" her mom asked.

"Well, he said that the ghost appeared for the first time before the hotel was even open. In fact, it appeared before it was even finished being built."

"Really?" her mom leaned closer. "Go on."

Her dad laughed. "You're as bad as your daughter," he said.

"As *good* as," her mom corrected, wrinkling her nose at him. Then she turned back to Tabby. "Go on."

Tabby glanced at her notes. "Well, apparently the first sighting is pretty well known. I heard a bit about it from April. About a month before the hotel opened, so—sometime in May 1951, there were a bunch of men who had been working in the ballroom—doing the floors or something. They were gathering up their things, getting ready to go home, and they were all singing."

"Singing?"

Tabby's dad grinned. "You know the song! Heigh-ho, Heigh-ho! It's home from work we go!"

Her mom slapped her dad in the arm and rolled her eyes, then looked back at Tabby. "What were they singing?"

"Mr. Withers didn't remember," Tabby said. "He just said they were singing. And suddenly, the ghost was standing there, looking at them." She shrugged. "I guess they were pretty scared. A lot of them ran and some even fainted. Most of them could never be convinced to come back; even those who had been working in other parts of the hotel. They just left. Some didn't even collect their pay."

"Well, I can imagine that it must have been pretty frightening," her mom said. "Makes me shiver to think about it."

"Come here. I'll protect you," her dad said.

"Ri-ght." Her mom grinned.

"Anyway, after that, the ghost was seen a lot."

"When there was music playing."

"Usually," Tabby said. "A couple of times, people working in the ballroom thought they saw something in the mirror, but when they turned around, it was gone."

"Like when you thought you saw the ghost when your father and I were dancing," her mother said.

"Yeah. Like that. Actually—" she stopped.

"What?" her mom said.

"Nothing. Just thinking."

"Oh. Well. Did Mr. Withers know anything more?"

"Nope. Just that the ghost started appearing then and has been appearing ever since."

"So this hotel opened for business in 1951," her dad said.

"Yeah. In June of 1951," Tabby said. "They had a great ball. All the richest people in the area came to it."

"And the ghost?"

"Yeah, it was there; dancing with the rest."

"I'll bet that caused a stir!" her mom said.

"Yeah, it did. But well, by that time, people had heard a lot about the ghost and lots of them were there hoping to see her. But it still caused a panic and there were people running around and screaming and stuff. One woman even got knocked down and broke some ribs."

"People are weird," her mom said.

Her dad grinned at her mom. "What are you talking about, Rose? You'd give anything to be able to see the ghost!"

Her mom rolled her eyes and shrugged. "You're right," she said, sheepishly.

"Anyway, if it was a ghost they wanted to see, they got their wish," her dad said.

Tabby shrugged. "I agree with mom. People are weird."

Her mother laughed. "This, from the girl who practically camped out in the halls of the Banff Springs, hoping for a glimpse of a ghost?"

"Well. Maybe they're just spirits of girls who have died and have—unfinished business," Tabby said.

Her parents stared at her. "Girls? Unfinished business?" her dad said.

"Yeah. I think our ghost is a girl. And maybe she just wants help."

Her dad shrugged. "We can make all sorts of guesses, Tabs. We'll never really know."

"Yeah, I guess you're right." Tabby said. She rubbed her eyebrow. "Sooo—what's for dinner?"

Chapter 7: Where Tabby Collects More Memories. And Makes More Friends. Also Not Her Age.

"That's all he knows?" Beth said. *"When I first appeared? I could have told you that!"*

It was early the following morning and they were in Tabby's room. Tabby was feeling irritated and impatient. She hadn't gotten much sleep. "Well why didn't you, then?" She turned on her side and pulled the covers up over her shoulder. "I'm having a really tough time here!"

"I am sorry," Beth said. *"I spoke without thinking."*

"Yeah, well, I'm doing my best."

"Of course you are."

"Besides, you didn't know the date or anything."

"That is true."

"Basically, all you knew was that you are a girl. And you didn't bother to share that till I asked."

Beth let out a sigh. *"You are right, my friend."*

Tabby sighed too. "I'm sorry," she said, sitting up and pulling the covers up to her chest. "I shouldn't take it out on you. Last night I just didn't—never mind." She stretched and scratched her shoulder blade. "So we at least have a starting point. The hotel opened in the summer of 1951. You were first seen a month before. In May."

"May!" Beth said. *"I love May!"*

"So you can remember the month of May."

"Yes."

"But you can't remember anything else."

Beth shrugged transparent shoulders. *"Well, May has nothing to do with my death."*

"It is probably the month you died," Tabby told her.

"Oh."

"So now where do we go?" Tabby asked.

"Well, what about the people who were there in those early days?" Beth asked.

Tabby looked at her. "Beth, that was sixty years ago! Most of them are probably in senior's homes. Or dead."

"Oh. Of course."

Tabby frowned. "I guess I could ask."

"Who?"

"Well, maybe April could remember something else."

"The lady who looks after all of the parties?"

"Yeah. They say she knows the most about the ghost," Tabby said. "I mean you."

"Let's ask her!" Beth said excitedly.

"By *let's*, I take you mean *me*?"

* * *

"Hello, my dear! What brings you in here today?" April was in the laundry, helping a couple of girls fold snowy, white tablecloths.

"Just wanting to know more about the ghost," Tabby said.

"Have a seat."

Tabby looked around. There were no chairs. Several tables were piled high with clean laundry waiting to be folded. "I'll keep busy while we talk," she said, moving to a table and reaching for a towel.

April smiled at her. "You're a good girl." She watched as Tabby snapped the towel and expertly folded it. "And you've had training."

Tabby shrugged. "Just spent all of my life in hotels."

April laughed. "Well, it shows!" She grabbed another cloth. "So what do you want to know today?"

"Well, I've heard that the first time B—the ghost was seen, it was in the ballroom."

"That's right, Kitten," April said. "A group of workers just finishing for the day."

"And they were singing."

51

"Right, again."

"What I was wondering was—are any of them still around?"

"Oh, definitely," April said.

"They must be very old."

"Well not so very old, Kitten." April smiled. "One of them is my husband."

Tabby stared at her. "Really? Your husband?"

"Right, Kitten." April's smile widened. "He is a bit older than me, but not that much."

"Oh, wow! I mean—umm—good," Tabby said. "Is there any way I can talk to him?"

"Oh, he'd love to talk to you. How about now?"

"Like, *right* now?"

"No better time. Here, let me finish with these tablecloths and I'll take you to see him."

Tabby looked around. "Does he work here, too?"

April picked up another tablecloth. "Oh, he used to, Kitten. He was the head carpenter for many, many years. But his arthritis started acting up a decade or so ago and he decided that making clocks would be his new great passion."

"So where is he?"

"He has a little workroom fixed up at our cottage down in the village."

"Oh." Tabby had been so interested in exploring the hotel and solving Beth's mystery, she hadn't even thought about the village, let alone set foot in it. "Maybe I'd better check with my Mom before I leave the hotel."

"You do that, Kitten and I'll finish up here. Meet me down in the car park."

"Okay!" Tabby took the elevator to her family's suite. "Mom!"

Her mother looked up from the computer. "Oh, Tabby Cat, you won't believe this! I just found my Great-Great-grandfather!" She seemed pretty excited. Tabby understood a bit. Her mother *had* been hunting for her elusive grandparent since forever.

"Umm—that's nice, Mom." Tabby summoned up a smile of congratulation.

"Well, a little more enthusiasm would be in order, I think," her mom said indignantly. "Come and meet him!"

Tabby rolled her eyes. She had been invited to 'meet' some of her ancestors before but 'meeting' them was not really what one did. Dutifully, she exclaimed over a name on a line. Then, "Mom!"

"What is it, dear?" her mother said, already turning the pages of a book at her elbow.

"Is it all right if I go with April to their cottage? Her husband knows more about the ghost!"

"April from Events?"

"Yeah. The old lady who looks after the parties."

"Oh, that would be fine, dear. Just be back in time for dinner."

Tabby darted back out into the hall, shutting the door on the sound of clicking computer keys.

The elevator was where she had left it, doors ajar, and she stepped in and pushed the car park button.

"*So was April any help?*"

Tabby jumped slightly and looked over at Beth who was standing against the back wall. "You know, I must be getting used to this," Tabby said. "You don't even scare me—much—anymore."

"*Well I never wanted to in the first place!*" Beth said indignantly.

"Anyway, yes. April's husband was with those men who were in the ballroom when you first appeared."

"*Oh, that is exciting!*" Beth said. "*I wonder if he knows anything.*"

"We'll soon see," Tabby said.

"*Let me know,*" Beth said. She started drifting up toward the ceiling.

Tabby was watching her. "That must be so fun!" she said.

"*What?*"

"Flying."

"*It's not really flying,*" Beth told her. "*It's more like—floating. Like in a dream.*"

"I still think it would be fun," Tabby said.

Beth shrugged and let herself sink slowly through the floor to her waist. She tilted her head back. "*You should try this!*" she said. Then disappeared completely.

"Show off!" Tabby muttered.

Somewhere below the floor, she heard Beth giggle.

The doors slid open and Tabby stepped into the brightly lit car park.

"Oh, there you are, Kitten!" April's cheerful voice echoed among the cars and pillars. "Are you ready?"

Tabby spotted the elderly woman on the far side, standing beside a small car in the employees section. She hurried over. "Yep. I'm here!"

"Well get in! I'm sure Walt will be happy to see you!"

For an elderly woman, April drove fast. In only a few minutes, she was pulling into the drive of a small, neat cottage. She stopped the little car and stepped out. "Walt!" she hollered. "I've brought someone to meet you!" She urged Tabby ahead of her up the walk.

The front door opened and a stooped, old man with a thick mop of snowy white hair peered at them between his spectacles and a bushy pair of brows. "Why, April! You're getting younger every day!"

"That's because you're looking at Tabby!" April said. "I'm the old woman in the rear!"

The old man laughed and held out a rough, work-worn hand. "Welcome, my dear," he said, shaking Tabby's hand gently. "Come in. Come in. Let me show you my clocks!"

April laughed. "Oh, don't let him get started! You'll never get out of here!"

Tabby looked from the one laughing face to the other. "You remind me of my parents," she said.

Walt raised his eyebrows. "Really? Is it because we're so spry and youthful?"

"Ummm--yes, that would be it," Tabby said, grinning.

The elderly couple laughed merrily.

Then, "Come. Let's get acquainted," Walt said. "I was just sitting down to tea."

He led Tabby through a tiny, spotless front room, with space enough only for a small couch and matching chair, one end table and a lamp.

From there, they entered a kitchen that wasn't much bigger, though it was bright and sunny with a small table set with a plate of brownies and a tea service. A kettle steamed sociably on the stove.

"While you're here, can we interest you in a cuppa?" April said. "Walt makes a mighty good cup of tea."

"I don't drink tea, thanks," Tabby said.

"Well, we have some juice. Or plain old water, if you'd prefer."

"Juice would be nice, thank you."

"Walt, if you would do the honors—" April said.

"Walt's getting the 'company' chair," Walt said as he disappeared through the far doorway.

April laughed and went to the fridge.

A short time later, with Tabby safely seated, the three of them sipped at their respective drinks.

Walt sat back and peered at Tabby. "So, Tabby, April tells me that your family has settled in quite well up at the hotel."

"Well, we certainly like it there," Tabby said.

"And, from early reports, the staff likes your dad."

Tabby smiled. "That's good."

"I understand he'd been out of work for a time," April said.

"Well, yes," Tabby told them. "He got sick and couldn't work for about a year. Then, once he was better, there weren't any senior management spots available."

Walt nodded. "It can be a tough market to break into at that level. Or to break *back* into."

Tabby nodded. "He sorta wondered if the reason this job was available was because the hotel is haunted."

April looked at Walt.

"Well, they sure seem to have a time keeping staff," he said. "I don't know if it's because of the isolation, or the ghost."

"People are spooked by anything they don't understand," April added.

"Well, I can't believe it's the ghost!" Tabby said. "She's—" her voice trailed off.

"*She?*" April said.

"Um—yes—*she*," Tabby said.

"It appears that you know more than the rest of us already," April said, smiling.

Tabby shrugged. "Oh that's—just my theory. I was just thinking—" she stopped again.

"About—?"

"Nothing." Tabby frowned. Keeping secrets was sometimes hard work.

Walt and April were silent for a moment, waiting for Tabby to continue. When she didn't, April finally spoke up. "Tabby is trying to learn more about our ghost."

"Really!" her husband said. "Well you've come to the right place! I was one of the first people to see her."

Tabby nodded. "I heard about that. Can you tell me about it?"

"I'd love to! Let me see--" Walt closed his eyes. "Let me just think back--"

"Oh, for heaven's sake, you remember it like it was yesterday!" April said.

Walt laughed and popped his eyes open once more. "I do," he said, grinning.

"So tell us, before Tabby dies of old age!"

Walt chuckled. "Well, it was a strange day all around," he said. "Mostly because of Mr. Withers."

"Mr. Withers?"

"Yes. He had been upset and impatient most of the day. He had hollered at several of the men for no real reason and had even instructed the foreman to fire one man who hadn't shown up to work."

"That wasn't like him?" Tabby asked.

"Oh, my, no! He was the friendliest young fellow."

"Young?" Tabby wrinkled her nose. "Of course he was," she added. "It's hard to think of him as anything but old."

"I understand," Walt said, grinning. "But, believe me, Mr. Withers was a young, strong fellow," Walt said. "In his late twenties, but already financially secure."

"He was rich then?"

"I think it had something to do with selling the family ranch," Walt said. "We never really got the whole story. His parents were killed and he was their only child. That sort of thing."

"Oh."

"He was only a couple of years older than me, but already married and with a wife and little girl."

"He had a family?"

"Yes, my dear. A beautiful young wife and their daughter."

"But where are they now?"

"Well, it was pretty tragic," Walt said. "The wife fell off the balcony of their penthouse and died instantly. The little girl was—I think she was sent to live with some relatives."

"That is sad. To have all of his family taken from him." Tabby thought about her own father and how near she and her mom had come to losing him.

"It was. For weeks, he just sort of—wandered around."

"But he perked up when it was time to open the hotel," April said.

"Yeah. At least he appeared to," Walt said. "He never really was the same again, though. He stopped laughing and became much as you see him today."

"Sad," April said.

"Sad?" Tabby looked at her. "I just thought he was grouchy."

"Couldn't you tell, Kitten? That man is as sad as you can get and still keep living."

"Oh." Tabby was silent for a moment. Then, "Can you tell me any more about that day?"

Walt grinned. "Going to keep my nose to the grindstone, are you?"

Tabby frowned. "Grindstone?"

"It's a figure of speech, Kitten," April said, her eyes twinkling. "Usually only used by old guys."

"Old guys!" Walt snorted.

"Go on, Old Guy," April said, laughing.

Walt rubbed a hand across his chin and frowned. "A couple of things stand out. Weird little things. I remember there were a couple of guys missing from the bus when we left the village to come to work, which was very unusual. It was the first time anyone had failed to show up through the whole project. We were all so grateful to have work." He shrugged. "One of the guys turned up all right, though. When the bus got to the hotel, he was already busy in the ballroom."

"What about the other guy?"

"That was another thing. He never did show up. He was the one that Mr. Withers fired later that day. We all thought it was strange because he and Mr. Withers had been pretty good friends."

"Huh." Tabby frowned, then looked back at Walt. "You said a *couple* of things were weird."

He nodded. "That guy? The one who was working when we got to the hotel that day? Well, when we saw the ghost, everyone was pretty startled and upset. But *he* went into hysterics. Then fainted dead away. Couldn't none of us revive him. Severe shock, I guess. We had to call an ambulance and he never came back to work after that, either."

Walt shook his head. "The next day, young Mrs. Withers had that accident. People started talking about curses and stuff. They closed the site down for a couple of days."

"Then Mr. Withers came to each of us and asked if we would return to work. He looked so sad and broken that some of us did. Enough of us that we were able to get things finished for the opening."

"Wow," Tabby said.

Walt nodded. "Yeah. Things were pretty crazy for a while here. But they settled down and went along smoothly. Well, except for the occasional ghost sighting."

"So does anyone know who the ghost is?"

Walt shook his white head. "No. It is always dressed in that drape thing and no one has ever been able to see its face."

"*Her* face, Walt," April said.

"Huh?"

"Tabby thinks it's a girl."

"Oh. Right." Walt looked at Tabby. "That's about all I can remember. I saw the ghost a few times while I was still working, but I haven't seen *her* now since I retired."

April laughed. "You probably wouldn't be able to see her now if she was standing right in front of you."

Walt grinned and took off his glasses, polishing them with a handkerchief he pulled from his pocket. "You're probably right, my dear."

April glanced at the clock. "Well, it's time for me to start supper. Would you care to join us, Tabby?"

"Oh!" Tabby, too glanced at the clock. "I have to go. Mom told me I could come if I got back in time for dinner."

"Well, I'll take you back then, Kitten," April said. "Come with me."

Walt got to his feet. "So nice to visit with you, my dear. Come back any time. We'd love to chat some more."

"If you remember anything else, you will tell me, won't you?" Tabby asked.

Walt extended his hand and shook hers warmly. "My dear, I'll do exactly that!"

 Chapter Eight: Where Tabby Mans the Desk. Again. And Gets Scared by Mr. Withers. Again.

Tabby followed April out to her car and a short time later, was walking through the door of her family's suite.

"I'm home!" she said.

Her mother set a steaming platter on the table and smiled at her. "Get washed up, Tabby Cat. Your dad is on his way."

"So how was your day, Tabs?" her father asked a few minutes later as he speared a piece of chicken from the plate his wife handed him.

Tabby shrugged. "Oh, it was fine."

"Tabby went with April, you know, from Hotel Events," her mother said.

Her dad grinned. "I like her. She's one of those cheerful people who are so easy to be around."

"She was very nice to me," Tabby said. "She took me to meet her husband, Walt."

"I understand he was the cornerstone of the carpentry shop here for nearly sixty years," her dad said.

"Well, to hear him tell it." Tabby grinned.

"Did you have a nice visit, dear?" her mom asked.

"I did," Tabby said. "They were telling me about the first day the ghost appeared."

Her dad raised his eyebrows. "Interesting stuff," he said.

"It was. Did you know that Mr. Withers had been married?" Tabby asked.

Her parents looked at each other.

"Well, I did," her dad said at last.

"It was so sad," Tabby said. "His wife fell off the balcony of their penthouse while the hotel was being built."

"And Mr. Withers sent their little girl to live with relatives," her dad said.

Her mom's eyes filled with tears. "Oh, that is sad." She reached for her husband's hand and gave it a squeeze. "Imagine that!"

"Walt and April said Mr. Withers is gruff because he lost everything." Tabby scraped rice off the serving spoon and onto her plate.

Her dad nodded. "I had pretty much arrived at the same conclusion."

"I don't know if I could go on after something like that," her mom said.

Her husband looked at her. "Nor I." Her parents exchanged a look.

Finally, her mom turned back to Tabby. "So, did April's husband say anything more?"

"Well he said there were a couple of strange things that happened that day."

"Really?"

Tabby told them about the missing men and the one who had come to work early and later fainted.

Her dad shook his head. "Well, there's no accounting for people. Some just can't handle a shock."

"Well, that guy sure couldn't," Tabby said. "Walt says he never came back afterwards, either."

Her mom reached for the bowl of buttered vegetables. "Probably too embarrassed."

Her dad shrugged. "Seems a pretty flimsy excuse to give up a good job."

"Walt says a lot of guys never came back," Tabby said. "Even though there weren't many jobs around here back then."

Her mom shook her head. "Superstition."

"Yeah. After Mrs. Withers died and the ghost appeared, they started to talk about the hotel being cursed."

Her mom grabbed her dad's arm. "Do you suppose the ghost is really Mrs. Withers?!"

"I thought of that, too," Tabby said. "But the ghost appeared before Mrs. Withers died, so I guess not."

"Oh. Of course."

Her dad pushed his plate away. "Well, that was delicious, dear," he said, leaning across and giving his wife a lingering kiss.

"Oh, thank you!" her mom blushed.

"Geeze, you two!" Tabby said, rolling her eyes.

Her parents grinned at her.

Tabby sighed. "You know, April and Walt reminded me of you two."

"Really?"

"Yeah. I told them that and they said it was because they were so young and--I think the word he used was--spry. Whatever that means."

Her parents laughed. " 'Active' pretty much sums it up," her mom said.

Tabby twisted her mouth. "Okay."

They laughed again.

"So, to get back to Tabby's mystery, what do we know so far?" her dad asked.

"Well . . ." Tabby started counting on her fingers. "One, we know that the ghost first appeared in May, just before the hotel opened. And two, that several people saw her."

"And that many of them never came back," her mom put in.

"Yeah. That's three."

"And that Tabs thinks it is a girl," Tabby's dad said.

"Four."

"That's not much," her mom said.

"Well, we also know that the ghost has always appeared in the ballroom," Tabby said. "Until now," she added under her breath.

"What's that?" her Mom asked.

"Nothing."

"So, adding it all together--" her dad nodded.

"You're right," Tabby said, holding up her hand with her fingers splayed. "We don't know much."

* * *

The next afternoon, Tabby was leaning against the front counter, watching Jana tap a stack of papers against the counter to straighten them.

"You know, I was really ready to hate your dad when you guys arrived," Jana said.

Tabby raised her eyebrows. "Well, I'm glad you decided not to."

Jana gave an unladylike snort. "I was born and raised in the village and I thought I should have been promoted to General Manager instead of bringing in some *outsider*."

"Have you worked here long?"

"I've been here since I was fourteen. I worked as a server at the banquets and as a maid and in the laundries." She shrugged. "I went to the city for a couple of years of college, but I came back after I graduated." She sighed. "Ten years all together."

"Wow, that is a long time," Tabby said.

Jana shrugged. "Not long enough, obviously." She shrugged again. "But I've been watching your dad and he knows so much more than I do."

Tabby nodded. "He's pretty smart."

Jana smiled rather ruefully. "He is that. And very good at managing." She looked at Tabby. "Did you know he's organizing an auction to sell off a bunch of the junk in the attics?"

"He mentioned it a couple of times."

"Well, it's genius," Jana said. "We get rid of the stuff, and people who want a piece of the past are happy to cart it away."

Tabby grinned. "Everyone's happy."

"Exactly!" Jana finished tapping all sides of her little stack of papers. "Do you mind watching the front desk for a few minutes, Tabby? I need to get this document down to legal."

"Sure." Tabby slid off her stool and stood beside the counter. "Go ahead."

"I'll only be a minute." Jama hurried away.

Tabby reached for a stack of fliers and started arranging them into neat piles.

The phone rang suddenly and she jumped. Then she shook her head and picked it up. "Overlook Hotel," she said clearly.

"I need to make a booking," the caller said.

"Oh, certainly, I'd be happy to help you with that."

Propping the receiver expertly between her cheek and shoulder, Tabby completed the booking and cradled the phone.

"You! Little girl! What's your name again?"

Tabby looked up and felt her eyes widen.

Mr. Withers was standing in front of her.

"Umm—Tabby, sir," she said shakily.

"Why are you manning the counter?"

"I'm just here for a moment while Jana runs some papers down to legal."

"I'll have her job for this!" Mr. Withers said, angrily.

"Oh, don't do that, Mr. Withers! It's okay, I can handle things."

He pursed his lips and looked at her. "I noticed. I was watching you."

Tabby felt her face grow warm.

"You handled that reservation like a pro."

"Well, I've been doing it for a long time," Tabby said.

He shook his head. "I thought you were just a useless little girl."

"I am a little girl, but I'm not useless!" Tabby said hotly.

Mr. Withers stared at her, then grew thoughtful. "You know, you remind me of—someone—"

"Someone young and spry?" Tabby said, smiling.

His almost smiled back. He pressed his lips together. "Well, young. But you do remind me of her."

"Who?"

"My daughter."

Tabby took a breath. "Your daughter looked like me?"

"Well, didn't look like you precisely. But she did have her mother's long, light-coloured hair. And she often wore it in a braid. Like you. And she was about your size. When she—left."

"How old was she?" Tabby asked. "When she went to live with your relatives."

"Eleven."

"Don't you ever see her?" Tabby asked.

He stared at her. "I—no—I—I don't. It's probably better this way."

"Oh, that's sad."

"It is." Mr. Withers sighed, then peered at Tabby. "I won't fire Jana today, but I'm going to speak to her about abandoning her post."

"Yes, sir," Tabby said.

"And talk to her about putting little girls in charge!"

"Yes sir," Tabby said again, grinning.

* * *

"Oh, sorry!" Tabby shrank back from the doorway to April's tiny office. She had waited until Jana returned and then come to visit with her friend.

April looked up from her desk. "Oh, come in, Kitten. Mr. Withers and I are done."

Tabby walked hesitantly into the room.

"You sure you've got all of that?" Mr. Withers said.

April looked back at the frail man standing beside her desk, then at a pad of paper in front of her. "Oh, yes, Mr. Withers, I've got it."

He nodded and turned to go. "We meet again, Miss Pillay," he said as he walked past her to the door. He stopped and turned. "You didn't leave the desk unmanned, did you?"

"Umm—no, sir," Tabby said. "I waited until Jana came back."

"Good girl." Mr. Withers disappeared.

April was smiling at her. "Well, that's a first!"

Tabby frowned. "First what?"

"The first time I've ever seen him talk to one of the children here. Heaven knows we get enough of them staying here. Dozens, sometimes. But he never acknowledges them."

"Huh." Tabby shrugged. "He says I remind him of his daughter. Before she left."

April looked surprised. "His daughter? He actually mentioned her?"

Tabby nodded. "He says I don't exactly look like her, but that I am about the same size and have the same colour hair."

"This is a first!" April frowned. "Wait. He says that you are about the same size?"

"Yeah. Before she went to live with relatives."

"Hmm," April said. "I never arrived on the scene until about two years after all of this happened. But the way everyone who knew her talked, I always thought that his little girl was— little. About two or three years old. I never realized that she was already a young lady." She shook her head. "Funny that he would send her away after his wife died when she really didn't need to be baby sat."

Tabby shrugged. "Maybe he just felt he couldn't do everything."

"Well, raising kids is no picnic," April said, grinning. "And it really is a two-person job, though a lot of people manage with just one. But his daughter no longer needed to be constantly watched over. She could more or less look after herself." She shook her head. "I guess no one really knows what goes on in another person's life. Right?"

"No," Tabby said. "I mean yes. Sorry. What was the question?"

April laughed.

* * *

"*He scares me.*"

Tabby laughed. Beth had been waiting as she left April's office. Now the two of them were sitting on the back stairs.

Well, Tabby was sitting. Beth had assumed the position, but was actually hovering just above the step.

"It always surprises me when I hear you say that," she said. "Imagine, a ghost being scared of the living."

"*Well, I am,*" Beth said. "*He always looks so—fierce.*"

"April and my parents think he is just really sad," Tabby said.

Beth was silent for a moment. "*Sad. Mad. They look the same to me.*"

Tabby shrugged. "I guess they do," she said. "Because I thought the same thing."

"*You don't anymore?*"

"Well, I had a bit of a talk with him and he was almost—nice."

"*Really?*"

"Yeah. April says he's nice--in a scary sort of way."

"*So we're back to scary,*" Beth said.

Tabby grinned. "Yeah." She frowned. "The thing is—I think he knows more about everything here in the hotel than he is saying." She sighed. "That means I'm going to have to talk to him again."

"*Well, better you than me,*" Beth said. "*He scares me.*"

Tabby laughed.

"Tabby, Kitten, who are you talking to?"

Tabby looked up. "Oh, April, you scared me," she said, putting a hand over her heart.

"Sorry, Kitten," April smiled. "Maybe if I wore a bell—?"

Tabby laughed. "What was it you asked me?"

"I was just wondering who you were talking to."

Tabby looked around, but wasn't surprised to find that Beth had disappeared again. "Just—umm—singing to myself," she said.

"It sounded more like speaking."

"April. Haven't you heard of 'rap' music?"

"Oh that!" April laughed and shook her head. "Yes. And I wish I hadn't. Anyway, I just got a phone call. Walt has remembered some more things and would like to talk to you."

"I'll go ask my Mom!" Tabby jumped to her feet.

"Meet you by the car," April said.

# Chapter Nine: In Which Tabby's Circle of Old Friends Grows Larger. And Older.

"So I've been thinking a lot about things since our last visit," Walt said, setting his teacup down and dabbing his lips with a snowy napkin.

Tabby set down her glass and looked at him expectantly.

"And one thing came to me."

"Go on, dear," April said. "I'm dying of curiosity." She looked at Tabby. "He refused to tell me about it until he had you here. It's been a long day."

Walt laughed. "Okay. Okay," he said, holding up his hands defensively. "I was thinking about the guy that was already at work when we got there that morning. It was curious because he didn't own a car or a bicycle and always rode the bus. Yet there he was. I suppose he could have hitched a ride with someone, but at that hour of the morning, it seems—unlikely."

April was silent for a moment. Then she frowned. "Doesn't seem like very big news."

Walt grinned. "Maybe not to you."

April snorted.

"I was also thinking about the other guy," Walt went on. "The one who didn't show up that morning. And then I remembered something. Did you know that he was originally Mr. Withers' partner?"

"Really?" Tabby said. "Partner?"

"Yep. They were pretty good friends. The fellow had originally come onto the site as his partner. But something happened and he had to sign over his interest to Mr. Withers. Then he remained on site as a foreman."

"That must have been embarrassing for him," April said.

"Well, I guess it would for most people, but he wasn't that kind of guy. He was the happiest, nicest guy in the world." He frowned. "I remembered a conversation I overheard between him and Mr. Withers. Mr. Withers was trying to keep him on as a partner and he refused. Said that without his money, he couldn't do it. I think it was shortly afterward that Mr. Withers offered him the foreman job."

"How sad."

"He didn't think so. I remember the first day he joined us as our crew foreman. He just smiled and shrugged his shoulders and said something like, 'The Lord giveth and the Lord taketh away'."

"That's a real scripture, Walt, you heathen!" April said.

"Is it? I thought I remembered it from somewhere." Walt grinned. "Anyways, he just worked from then on with us. Cheerful as could be."

"A rare man indeed," April said.

Tabby nodded. "He sounds nice. And no one ever saw him again after that day?"

"Nope," Walt said. "Not even a peek."

"Didn't anyone get curious?" April asked. "Look for him?"

Walt shrugged. "Not that I know of. He had no family. He was friendly with everyone, but after that first ghost sighting and the death of the Missus, everything was so confused. Men quit on the spot and never returned. Oh, I admit that most of them were still living in the village, but a few moved. He probably did the same."

"But where was he living?" April asked.

"I don't know," Walt said, frowning. "Most of us single guys were staying at Mrs. Frazier's Boarding House just down from the town hall." He vaguely waved one hand. "But I have no idea where he lived."

"Is it still there?" Tabby asked.

"What, Kitten?" April asked.

"Mrs. Whoozit's Boarding House."

"Mrs. Frazier's," Walt said, grinning. "No. Well, the building is, but it's a senior's lodge now."

"Do you think we could go and see it?"

April shrugged. "I don't see why not," she said. "It would do Walt some good to get some fresh air anyway."

Walt looked at her. "What are you talking about? I walk clear to the end of the driveway every single day!"

"Right," April grinned. "What is that? Thirty steps?"

"Thirty-two, but who's counting?" Walt said, returning his wife's grin.

"Come on, old man, let's take Tabby for a walk about the village," April said.

* * *

"This used to be Mrs. Frazier's Boarding House." Walt stopped on the sidewalk and looked across the wide lawn toward a large, brick building. "She was the wife of a rich man, and this had been her home. But after he died, she took in boarders and ran a pretty fancy place."

"Did you stay here?" Tabby asked.

"For a short, wonderful while. Till I got married." He smiled. "The meals were amazing!"

"Humph!" April said.

"Oh, nothing like yours, my dear," Walt said quickly.

"Right," April huffed.

Walt laughed.

"Walt, you old nail-pounder! Is that you?"

They all looked toward the former boarding house.

An elderly man was just being wheeled out onto a wide porch. He leaned forward. "It *is* you! I can't believe you're still alive!"

"Ted! You sorry excuse for a carpenter! How are you?" Walt started up the brick walk.

"I can't complain," Ted said. "Well, I could, but no one would listen anyway!"

Both men laughed.

Walt slowly climbed up the two steps to the porch and reached out a gnarled hand. It was tightly gripped by his friend in the wheelchair.

Tabby stood to one side as the three elderly friends spent some time getting re-acquainted.

Finally, Ted looked around. "I've come full circle," he said. "I'm back at the boarding house. I will say the meals aren't nearly what I remember."

"It would be hard to out cook Mrs. F," Walt said, grinning.

Ted peered over April's shoulder at Tabby. "Is this a granddaughter?"

Walt glanced around. "Oh, no, this is our young friend, Tabby. Her dad is the new GM over at the hotel."

April put an arm around Tabby's shoulders. "Well, she is like a granddaughter."

Tabby smiled.

"Tabby's been trying to find out about our ghost," April said. "We've been telling her what we know."

"Really!" Ted said. "Well, maybe I can help a bit."

Walt offered April and Tabby each a chair, then took one himself and turned to Tabby. "Ted used to live here in the early days. In fact, he was with me that day we first saw the ghost."

Tabby looked at the elderly man in the wheelchair. His head was completely bald and his skin hung from a frame that looked as though it had shrunk. But bright, black eyes sparkled at her beneath weedy eyebrows.

"Do you remember what happened?" Tabby asked.

"Well, my memory probably isn't up to Walt's standards," Ted said. "But I do remember some things."

"Ooh, what?" Tabby eagerly pulled her chair closer to the elderly man.

Ted laughed. "I can't tell you how long it's been since a young lady sat next to me."

"Just like old times, eh, Ted?" Walt asked.

"Really old times." Ted grinned.

Tabby stared. She had just realized he had no teeth.

He rubbed a hand over his chin. "Let's see. Well I remember that first sighting. We were just finishing our shift and one of the guys, Rolly, his name was, started singing." He looked at Walt. "Remember, Walt, what a fine voice he had?"

Walt nodded. "I remember, though I had forgotten his name till now. Rolly. Of course."

"Go on," Tabby said eagerly.

"Well, Rolly started singing and the rest of us joined in. Had some pretty good singers. You weren't bad if I remember correctly, Walt."

Walt just grinned and shook his head.

Ted smiled. "Anyway, we were singing and, suddenly, Rolly stopped. The rest of us looked at him and realized that he was staring at a small figure, standing beside him. His face had gone pale. Someone standing a ways away even joked about it. 'Rolly! You look like you've seen a ghost!' "

Ted shrugged. "Of course that's exactly what had happened. About then, one of the men started screaming and there was instant chaos."

"Most everyone ran out the big double doors into the front lobby area. Me and another fellow were trying to calm the screaming guy down. He finally gurgled something and then dropped like a stone."

"And was the ghost still there through all this?" Tabby asked.

"It sure was. Standing right there in the ballroom." Ted shivered. "I remember it like it was yesterday. Someone finally called the ambulance and it came over from Maryton. Took about half an hour and that guy was out the whole time. Once they took him away, we were able to get on the bus for the trip back to town."

"I remember that," Walt said. "It was a pretty excited group."

Ted nodded. "Yeah. They were either talking at the top of their voices or sitting there, stunned."

"How long was the guy in hospital?" Tabby asked.

"Well, that, I can't tell you," Ted said. "Because he never came back. In fact, about two weeks later, Mrs. F had a couple of us guys clean out his room, so she could rent it out to someone else. I guess he had checked out of the hospital and disappeared."

"Huh." Walt frowned. "So he was never seen again."

"Not that I ever heard," Ted said. "We stored his trunk in the attic, though, and it was still there when I moved out."

"So—the ghost appeared in the ballroom," Tabby said thoughtfully.

Ted nodded. "I could put an 'X' on the exact spot. It's that clear."

"And two guys disappeared."

"Yeah." Ted frowned. "I don't remember their names."

"Mr. Parker?"

Ted turned.

A young woman dressed in light blue scrubs was standing in the door. "I think you've had enough sun today."

Ted sighed. "My keepers summon me."

"Well, I'll be back, Ted," Walt said. "Now that I know you're here!"

"I'll look forward to it!" Ted grinned. "Nice to see you, April," he said as his aide pushed him inside. "And nice to meet you, Tabby!"

Walt got to his feet. "Well, that is a nice surprise," he said.

April took his arm as he negotiated the two steps to the walk. "It was nice to see Ted again."

A church bell started to chime.

"Oh-oh, noon," April said.

Tabby looked at her watch. "I'd better be getting back. Mom is planning on canning syrup this afternoon and she wants to get lunch out of the way quickly."

"What time was she expecting you?" April asked.

"12:30."

"Well, let's get Walt back to the house and I'll drive you."

Walt snorted. "As long as we're talking about Walt in the third person, Walt would like to go along for the ride."

April laughed. "Fine then. Let's take him."

Walt and April kept up a lively conversation till they reached the great front doors of the hotel.

"There you go, Kitten." April reached back to swing the door open. "We'll see you soon!"

"And I'll keep thinking," Walt said.

April elbowed him in the side. "I'll try to see that he doesn't hurt himself!"

"Hey!"

They both laughed.

Tabby shook her head and closed the door, then ran up the front steps. Stepping into the elevator, she punched the number of her family's floor.

"*How did you do?*" Beth's head poked up through the floor.

Tabby jumped to one side of the elevator. "Man, Beth. Don't do that!" she squeaked.

Beth emerged into the car. "*Sorry, Tabby. I just keep forgetting how things must look to the living.*"

"They look pretty screwed up when there are heads sitting on the floor," Tabby grumbled.

"*I am sorry. So what did you learn?*"

"Oh, just more about the guy who fainted and the one who disappeared. Not a lot more than I knew before. Things like where they lived and stuff. There is another old guy who is trying to help us."

"*You sure do know a lot of old people,*" Beth said.

"Yeah," Tabby said. "But, old people are the only ones who know anything about this." She looked at Beth. "Besides, if you had stayed alive, *you'd* probably be about seventy years old by now."

"*Seventy?!*"

"Yeah. And probably sitting on a porch swing with these other old people."

"*I never thought—*"

"So you'd better have some respect."

"*Oh, I meant no disrespect!*" Beth was quick to correct Tabby. "*I was just remarking that, for a young person, you are certainly surrounded by people—not your age.*"

"I know," Tabby said sadly. "My best friends are still back in Banff. I don't know anyone else."

"*Don't you ever get to know the young people who stay here?*"

"Well, they come and go so quickly that I really don't get the chance."

"*Oh, I am sorry.*"

"Actually, you know, I really don't think about it much anymore. In fact, I sort of like hanging out with the older people."

"*Well, that is good.*"

"So anyways, I'm still working on it," Tabby said. "But it's slow."

"*I thank you*," Beth said, melting away.

The doors opened, Tabby stepped out into the hall and a second later, she was opening the door to her family's suite.

"Mom?"

"Over here, Tabby Cat," her mother said as she lifted something out of an old trunk sitting against the dining room wall. She turned and set it on the dining room table.

Tabby joined her. "What's all this?"

The shining surface was littered with strange gadgets and stacks of yellowed papers.

"Oh, your dad found a couple of old trunks in the attic." Her mom waved a hand. "He thought there might be something that we can put into the auction."

"Wow! What's this?" Tabby lifted a heavy, metal, bell-shaped item by its large handle.

"That's a chopper, I think," her mom said.

"Chopper?"

"Used to chop vegetables. And maybe pastry."

"Wow! You'd end up with major muscles if you used this very often."

Her mother laughed.

"Huh," Tabby held up a small ladle-shaped object. "Let me guess. A strainer for really small amounts?"

"That's a tea-strainer," her mother said.

"Oh. Like I know what that is."

Her mom laughed. "Tea bags are a fairly recent invention. Tea leaves used to be scooped loose into the teakettle and when you poured out the tea, you had to pour it through a strainer or you'd end up with all of the leaves in your cup."

"Bleagh!"

"In a word!" Her mom nodded.

Tabby lifted a yellowed menu. "Wow look at this!" she said.

Her mother leaned over her shoulder. "Isn't that amazing?" she said.

"I can't believe the prices!" Tabby said, pointing. "Look at that. An entire meal for a dollar and a half!"

"You have to remember that people earned a lot less than they do now."

Tabby lay the menu down carefully and circled the table. "So people are interested in this stuff?"

"They certainly are," her mom said. "Some people have whole collections of antique kitchen memorabilia and gadgets."

"Good thing I'm not the one buying," Tabby said. "Or nothing would get bought."

"I'm with you. I like my modern conveniences," her mom said. "I think I'll stick with my electric gadgets." She straightened. "Ready for lunch?"

There was no answer.

"Tabby?"

Tabby was staring at the old trunk.

"Tabs?"

She looked at her mother. "Sorry. What?"

"I asked you if you were ready for lunch."

"Oh, yeah. Yeah, I'm starving. And it was this afternoon you wanted to can syrup, right?"

"That I do," her mom said. "So we're having lunch with your father down in the dining room."

"Goody!" Tabby said.

# Chapter Ten: In Which Tabby Goes Exploring—In The *yawn* Seniors' Centre Attics.

Tabby's dad leaned back in his chair and sighed happily. "Can you believe we've been here for one month today?" he asked.

"Has it really been a month?" her mom asked.

"Half of my summer holiday is gone," Tabby said sadly.

"But just think," her dad said. "In a few weeks, you will be going back to school and making a whole bunch of new friends."

"Yeah. That's really exciting," Tabby said sourly.

Her dad laughed. "Back to my original statement, yes, it's really been a month." He turned to Tabby, "And I'm really sorry that your holiday is half over."

"But that means I've only got a month to—" Tabby swallowed the rest of what she had been about to say.

"Coffee, Mr. Pillay?"

Tabby's dad looked up. "No, thank you, Doris. I'm not a coffee drinker. But please tell Mrs. White that dinner was delicious!"

"I will, thank you. Mrs. Pillay?" Doris smiled and held up the coffee pot again.

"I'm not much for coffee, either," Tabby's mom said.

"Tabby?"

"Ugh!" Tabby said.

"Tabby!" her dad frowned at her.

"Sorry!" Tabby blinked. "I meant, no thank you. I don't want any coffee."

Doris laughed and left.

"Tabby, you know better than that!" her mother said softly.

"I'm sorry! I was thinking about something else."

"In our position, we can't ever 'think about something else'," her dad said quietly.

"I know! I know! It won't happen again!"

"Good." Her dad got to his feet. "Well, I have to get back at it." He leaned over and gave his wife a kiss. "See you in a few hours."

"I'll probably be a sticky mess, but don't let that stop you," her mom said, grinning.

"I look forward to it!" her dad said. He gave Tabby a kiss on top of her head, then left the dining room.

"Well, slave, are you ready?" Her mom stood up.

Tabby followed her mother to the lobby. "You know, Mom, I've been thinking."

"Really?"

Tabby ignored her mother's smile. "Yeah. That man I told you about. Ted? Walt and April's friend? Well, he said that he and another guy packed up a third guy's stuff and stored it in the attic of the boarding house."

"I think I'm following you," her mother said. "And this has something to do with your ghost?"

"Well, it might," Tabby said. "This guy disappeared after screaming and fainting when he saw the ghost."

"Huh."

"Yeah. Ted said that he fainted after the ghost appeared and that they took him to the hospital. And that he was never seen again. No one knows where he went afterwards." She scratched her chin. "The thing is, Ted and this other man packed up his stuff in a trunk in the attic." She looked at her mother. "I wonder if that trunk is still there. And if it could tell us something."

Her mom stopped and looked at Tabby. "You want to go and poke around in some mouldy old attic?"

"Mom, it's a senior's home. I doubt if their attic is any worse than the one here."

Her mom shrugged. "You're probably right, Tabs." "But you'll have to make sure you get permission."

Tabby looked at her. "Well, of course I'll get permission. I know how these things work."

"And it'll have to wait until we get your Dad's syrup canned. Those chokecherries aren't going to process themselves."

* * *

"*What was that stuff?*" Beth asked.

"Chokecherry syrup," Tabby said, flopping down on her bed. She and her mom had just put the last batch of jars into their water bath. Tabby's job was done. She yawned. Housework was hard work. "And how do you know what I was doing? Were you watching?"

"*Always,*" Beth said.

"Really," Tabby sat up. "You watch me all of the time?"

"*Well not* all *of the time,*" Beth said. "*I do know that you need your privacy. But when you are doing interesting things, I watch.*"

"I do interesting things?"

"*To someone from my time, yes,*" Beth said.

"Huh." Tabby digested that. Then she looked at Beth. "Tell me, Beth, where, exactly *can* you go?"

"*You mean here in the hotel?*" Beth asked.

"Yes. And out of the hotel."

"*Oh, I can't go off hotel property,*" Beth said. "*I have to stay within the limits of the grounds.*"

"Really. Who makes these rules?" Tabby asked.

Beth stared at her. "*I have no idea,*" she said at last. "*I just know that I can't go outside of the hotel boundary.*"

"Weird," Tabby said. "But you can go anywhere inside the hotel?"

"*Oh, yes. I was up in the attics with you once.*"

"I remember that. You nearly startled me to death!"

"*I am sorry,*" Beth said. "*I don't mean to frighten. I forget how--unusual my appearance must be to the living.*"

"Unusual. Yeah. That's the word." Tabby grinned. She flopped back onto the bed and sighed.

"*So, I'm still curious about that syrup you were putting into bottles. What do you do with it?*"

"Huh?"

"*The - you called it - chokecherry syrup. What do you do with it?*"

"Oh. You eat it."

"*Really. What, like soup? With a spoon?*"

Tabby turned her head.

Beth was sitting cross-legged in the air beside the bed.

Tabby sat up again. "Beth, I'd give anything to know how you do that," she said.

Beth looked around. "*Do what?*"

"Sit there." Tabby pointed. "In the air!"

Beth laughed. "*Tabby, you know I can sit wherever I want. Remember? I'm the one who can float?*"

"Oh yeah, I know that. I just wish I knew *how* you do it," Tabby said, dropping back down onto her bed. "And that I could learn."

Beth sighed. A soft, hollow sound. "*Believe me, I would gladly give it up just to be able to do one little thing. Like--tie a shoe. Or hold a fork. Or--brush my hair.*"

"Do you have hair?"

"*Of course I have hair!*" Beth said indignantly. "*I think . . .*"

Tabby smiled. "I guess I need to start seeing things from your perspective."

Beth sighed. "*And I yours.*"

Tabby pushed herself to her feet. "Well, if I'm going to go down to the senior's home tomorrow, I need to make some arrangements."

"*I do wish I could go with you on some of these excursions.*"

Tabby made a face. "I wish you could, too."

* * *

Tabby and April had agreed that 1:00 the following afternoon was a good time to present themselves at the senior's home.

To Tabby, the wait was endless.

But finally, she and April were standing in front of a small, thin woman seated at a spotless desk. A brass plaque on the desk read, Ms. Franks, Home Supervisor.

"So what do you need that's so important?" Ms. Franks asked, folding her hands together on the top of her desk.

Tabby stared at her. Ms. Franks' skin was transparent and smooth and she didn't appear to have any lips. Light brown hair was scraped back severely into a bun at the back of her head, giving the impression that her highly-arched eyebrows had been pulled that way by her enthusiastic hairdo.

"We wondered if it would be all right if we had a look around in your attic," April said.

Ms. Franks pulled back slightly, her rather prominent blue eyes wide with surprise. "In our attic? What could you possibly want in our attic?"

"My friend, Tabby here—"

Tabby broke in. "I'm really interested in old stuff. At the— that is—we at the hotel have been going through the attics. At the hotel. Getting stuff out for the auction—you know—" she nodded toward a colourful poster tacked to the wall of the woman's office.

Ms. Franks' lipless mouth stretched into a semblance of a smile. "Oh, yes. The auction. The residents here are quite excited about it."

"Anyway, we're asking people in the village if they have anything they want to contribute. For charity."

"Well, you're welcome to look around." Ms. Franks got to her feet. "But I don't think you will find anything. The local antique shop owner went through there a couple of years ago and dragged out everything he thought was valuable."

Tabby's heart sank.

"Well, you never know," April said, brightly.

Ms. Franks shrugged. "I have no problem with you looking. Just so long as you're careful." She shivered slightly. "I've never been up there myself. I don't like pokey old places where there are no lights." She led them up the stairs to a door in the long, second-floor hall. "Just straight up here." She swung the door wide, disclosing a long flight of bare, wooden steps. "I think the caretaker keeps a light on the bottom step. Ah, yes." She pointed to an old-fashioned flashlight, then waited while Tabby lifted the heavy thing and clicked it on.

A long beam of light shot out into the gloom and Tabby pointed it up the staircase.

"Be careful," Ms. Franks said again.

"Oh, we will," April assured her as the two of them started up the creaking staircase.

April laughed. "Och! These stairs sound like me in the morning."

Tabby glanced behind her at the elderly woman. "Sounds like you need tightening."

"Ohh, I'd smack you if I could see!"

Tabby laughed as she stepped up onto the attic floor. "Careful here, April."

"I'll stick close, Kitten."

Tabby made her way slowly toward the faint light shining through a yellowed blind at the far end of the room. When she finally reached it, she put out a hand and pulled the string. The blind flipped up, letting in a long bar of midday light.

April looked around and put her hands on her hips. "Well, this is disappointing."

The room was mostly empty. Only a couple of sheet-draped pieces of furniture, pushed up against the wall, remained.

Tabby lowered the flashlight. "Rats! What do we do now?"

April started toward the draped pieces. "Well, let's not give up too easily. There might be something up here still."

The two of them pulled dust covers off a tall wardrobe with a warped back and two missing drawers, and a marble-topped washstand that was minus both its mirror and one leg.

Tabby tried to pull out the remaining drawer of the wardrobe, but it was stuck tight. She poked the flashlight through the space made by the missing drawers and peered down.

"Empty," she said, disgusted.

April opened the front doors of the washstand, then sat back and wrinkled her nose. "Well, there's something here."

Tabby hurried over. "What?" she asked.

"A mouse nest. A really old and smelly one."

Tabby made a face. "Great!"

"Let's walk around. See if there's anything else."

The two of them made a complete circuit of the floor, but found only a broken wooden crate and an ancient box of mouse poison.

Tabby sighed. "That antique dealer really cleaned this place out."

April nodded. "Frankly, I'm surprised the box of mouse poison is still here. People will buy almost anything old. This must have been a real treasure trove for him."

"Another idea shot to pieces," Tabby said. She looked at April. "What do you suggest now?"

"Well . . ." April frowned. "We could go to the antique shop and see if the dealer found anything."

Tabby shrugged. "I guess."

The two of them made their way back to the supervisor's office.

"Well, that didn't take long," Ms. Franks said.

Tabby sighed. "There wasn't anything up there."

"Yes," April added. "Your antique dealer pretty much cleaned the place out."

Ms. Franks shrugged. "Oh. Well, I'm sorry about that. I did tell him to take anything he thought was of value."

"Apparently everything was." Tabby smiled ruefully.

"We wondered if you could give us the name of that dealer," April said.

Ms. Franks nodded. "Sure. It's Henry Burbur. You know the guy? One street over." She pointed. "His shop is in his home. Just look for the sign, 'Old Henry's' ".

"Oh, I know Henry," April said. "Come on, Kitten!"

 ## Chapter 11: Where Tabby Searches Through Old Trunks and Dirty Laundry. Ugh.

The old man peered at them through the screen door. "Anything I can help you folks with?"

"Henry, it's me. April."

He pulled glasses from his pocket and put them on.

"Well, for heaven's sake. We live, what, three blocks from each other and I haven't seen you in months."

April laughed. "Shocking, isn't it!"

He unhooked the screen and Tabby heard the cheerful tinkle of a bell as he swung it wide. "Come in, ladies, come in. What can I do for you?"

Tabby and April stepped into a small vestibule, bare except for a single large framed photograph of two elderly people on the yellow-painted wall.

"We heard that you were the person who carted a load of junk out of the senior's lodge attics a couple of years ago," April told him.

Henry frowned and stared at her. "Junk out of the senior's attic?" Then his face cleared. "Oh. Oh, yes. Several loads. The supervisor there told me I could have it. As long as I took everything."

"You left a couple of things," Tabby said.

Henry looked at her and grinned. "Well, let's just say that I took everything that I could move. Or repair."

April laughed. "Well I don't blame you for not wanting that wardrobe. It's pretty far past any hope of repair."

"And the washstand was missing a leg," Tabby added.

Henry nodded.

"Did you find any trunks?" April asked.

"Trunks?" Henry rubbed his hand across a bristly chin. "There were a couple. I think I still have at least one. Do you want to have a look?" He didn't wait for an answer, but turned and led the way into the house.

April followed.

Tabby started after April, then stopped and blinked. Where she would have expected to see a living room or kitchen, there were rows of old furniture and display cabinets filled with—junk.

Henry turned and smiled at her. Waving a hand, he said, "Welcome to 'Old Henry's.'"

"Wow, Henry! You've really expanded!" April said.

Henry nodded and raised his eyebrows. "I like it."

"Tabby, look at this!" April walked over to an oversized travel case and carefully opened it. "This is what the wealthy used when they travelled."

"They did!" Henry grinned. "You see the jars and containers inside are lead crystal and silver. The wealthy spared no expense when they hit the road."

April carefully set down a jar she had picked up. "Too rich for me." She straightened. "So—the trunks? From the attic?"

Henry indicated the way with his head. "They're in the back storage room. Let's go and have a look, shall we?" He led the way past the neat rows to a double door in the back. "In here."

Tabby and April followed him through.

He snapped on the light and pointed to a couple of trunks shoved under a large shelving unit. "Those are the only two trunks left in the store right now. Other than the fancy one out front."

"Well, let's have a look," April said.

Henry pulled one of the trunks out to the middle of the floor, undid the clasps and carefully laid the heavy, curved lid back.

An empty tray, covered in faded pink, striped fabric, was easily lifted out.

Tabby and April leaned forward eagerly, but the rest of the trunk was empty.

"You can see that this trunk is in excellent condition." Henry pointed out several features. "There is no damage and little wear. Considering the age of the item—"

"Actually, we're more interested in contents than in the trunk itself," April said.

"Oh." Henry looked into the empty trunk. "Yes. Well—uh—strike one." He replaced the tray and closed the lid. He shoved the trunk back into its place and pulled out the other one, then carefully undid the single remaining clasp. "As you can see, this one's not in very good shape." He pushed back the lid, gentle with the rusty, weakened hinges.

There were papers and toiletries in the top tray.

"Ohh, look at that!" April said.

Henry lifted the tray out.

The trunk was full—with work clothes and boots on top.

Tabby's eyes widened.

Just then, the front door bell jingled. Henry straightened. "Oh, I'd better get that. Do you mind if I leave you two ladies here?"

"Fine with me," April said. "If you don't mind us snooping."

"Snoop away. But if you find anything valuable, it's mine!" He laughed and disappeared into the display room.

"How about you go through the tray, Kitten," April suggested. "I'll see what's in the bottom part."

"Okay." Tabby knelt down on the floor and carefully lifted out a stack of yellowed papers.

April pulled out the boots and trousers and laid them beside her. Beneath them were a jacket and an empty canvas bag. April added them to her pile on the floor. "Ugh. No wonder Henry never got around to unpacking this trunk," she said. "Someone's old laundry."

The canvas bag had been covering several pairs of soiled socks and underwear. She added them to the growing pile on the floor. "How are you doing, Tabby?"

Tabby looked up. "There are several letters here, to someone named Mike Plunkett. From January and February, 1951."

April glanced over at the letters in Tabby's hands. "Well, that's the right time period."

"Oh, here's another one from March. They're kinda hard to read."

"How about we trade jobs?" April moved closer to Tabby.

Tabby looked at the heap of old clothing. "Yuck."

April laughed and reached for the stack of letters.

Tabby made a face and handed them to her, then shuffled over to the trunk and peered hesitantly into it. "More clothes." She pulled out a stack of folded shirts and another of neatly-folded pants. "This stuff looks clean. Oh, here are some books and a clock."

Tabby set a large, wind-up clock on the floor, then stacked four books beside it.

"What's this? Oh." She ran a finger across the top of a large tin. "Tobacco," she read. She pried the lid open. "Ugh. It really *is* tobacco. What are these?" She held up a packet of small, white papers.

April looked up. "Oh, those are cigarette papers, Kitten. For rolling your own."

"Oh." Tabby made a face and pushed the lid back on. Then she set the tin beside the clock.

She leaned over the side once more, then sat back on her heels. "There are some more pairs of underwear in the bottom," she said. "They look like those old-fashioned long johns. You know? The ones with the trap door in the backside?"

"Is that all?"

"I think so. I really don't want to see."

April laughed. "The great investigator. Just a moment, Kitten and I'll have a look."

Tabby reached for some of the papers April had set on the floor. "Did you find out anything?"

April looked at her. "Well, I'm pretty sure this is our man. These letters are from an uncle and aunt in Manitoba. They were excited about his job building the new hotel and hoping that this would help him make a new start."

"A new start?"

April nodded. "Obviously, he had been struggling. At least financially. His aunt writes that she hopes he will soon be able to start paying off his debts." April held up another sheet of paper.

"And this is an unfinished letter to them. I'm assuming from the same man. Look at the beautiful handwriting. And the nice paper!"

"Huh." Tabby looked down at the papers in her hand. "Wow! Look at this, April. Here are some ads for new cars. Well, new in 1951." Tabby shuffled the papers. "And for a new house."

April leaned over. "Wow is right! Pretty fancy for someone who was deeply in debt." She shrugged. "Well, I guess he wouldn't have been the first person to go from bad to worse."

"So what did you find out?" Henry was back.

April looked up. "Well, we're pretty sure this is the trunk we were looking for. It belonged to someone named Mike Plunkett."

Henry frowned. "Don't recall the name. Relative of yours?"

April shook her head. "That's who these letters are addressed to. Tabby and I assume that the rest of the contents were his also."

"Oh, this clock is valuable," Henry said. "And these books. And a tobacco tin! Great!" He peered into the trunk. "Anything else?"

"Just some more old underwear." Tabby pointed.

Henry lifted it out. "Oh. What's this?"

At the very bottom of the trunk was a carved piece of wood. He held it up.

"That looks like a fancy table leg!" April said.

Henry nodded. "I think so, too." He pursed his lips, thoughtfully and tapped his chin with the piece of wood. "In fact, if I'm not mistaken, I think it is the missing leg from the washstand in the senior's home attic."

April stared at him. "Why on earth would someone have a leg from a washstand in his trunk?" She took it from him and turned it over in her hands.

Henry frowned. "Maybe as a weapon?"

"C'mon, Henry," April said. "Have you *ever* heard of a crime in this town?"

Henry shrugged. "You have a point." He stared at the table leg. "Why would someone pack a leg in his trunk?"

"Well, if this is the man we're searching for, and I think it is, we know that he couldn't have packed his own trunk," April said.

"No?"

"No. He disappeared and a couple of the guys in the boarding house packed it for the landlady and stored it in the attic."

Tabby touched the piece of wood. "So the leg must have been in his room and the guys just threw it in with the rest of his stuff?"

April nodded. "Makes sense. But we're back to the original question. Why on earth would he have a table leg?"

"Maybe the washstand was in his room at some point," Henry suggested.

"I doubt that," April said. "I'm sure indoor plumbing was installed in that house in about the thirties."

"Well, I'm stumped." Henry grinned. "But nothing surprises me anymore. If you had seen the things I have seen in people's homes—"

"I'd like to hear about that," April said.

"So would I," Tabby spoke up.

The front door bell jingled happily again.

Henry sighed. "Some other time, ladies?"

April's eyes sparkled. "Count on it." She looked at Tabby. "But for now, we'd better get you home."

Tabby nodded. "Thank you, Mr. Henry." Her eyes fell on the table leg, still clutched in April's hands. For some reason, it interested her. She reached for it. "Would you mind if we took the leg with us?"

Henry frowned. "No, not at all. But why?"

Tabby shrugged, her eyes on the leg. "I don't know. Maybe it'll give us a clue."

"And I'd like to take these letters, if I may?" April held up the bundle of letters, along with the unfinished one. "I may find a clue."

Henry shrugged. "Why not? But let me know if you do discover anything."

April laughed. "Will do!"

* * *

Tabby said a hurried good-bye to April at the hotel entrance and rushed to her room. Then she laid the table leg on her bed, and started to scramble through the boxes in her closet.

Her mother stopped in the doorway, a stack of neatly-folded towels in her arms. "Don't tell me you are finally going to unpack the rest of your boxes!"

Tabby poked her head out. "Nope," she said cheerfully. "I'm just looking for my magnifying glass."

"Your what?"

"You know. From my old science set." She disappeared back into the closet.

"Tabby, what is this old table leg doing on your bed?"

"That's what I need the magnifying glass for!" Her voice had become muffled. She sneezed.

Her mother laughed. "I'm just going to walk away now."

"Oh, here it is!" Tabby pulled the box out into her room. *"So, why do you need a magnifying glass?"*

Tabby looked up.

Her mother was gone and Beth had taken her place beside the bed.

"Oh. Hi, Beth. I need the magnifying glass to examine that table leg."

Beth looked down. *"This table leg?"*

"Well, it's the only one in my room," Tabby's voice was muffled as she again stooped over her box.

"Oh. Yes, of course."

"Aha! Here it is!" Tabby held up her right hand. Tightly clutched in her fingers was a large, round magnifying glass.

Beth sat down in the air near the bed. *"Do you mind if I watch?"*

Tabby glanced at her, then shook her head. "Not at all. This concerns *you*, doesn't it?"

Beth nodded, then watched silently as Tabby sat down, picked up the wooden leg and laid it across her lap. She put the glass to her eye and bent over.

90

"*What are you looking for?*" Beth asked.

"I don't know. Clues."

"*Oh.*" Beth was silent.

Tabby peered carefully through her glass. The table leg was smooth and square at the very top, where it had originally been fastened to the table. Then the pictures started. Delicate flowers and birds had been carved into the beautiful wood. Tabby followed the leg from the top to the bottom. Then she flipped it to the next quarter and repeated the process.

"*Anything?*" Beth asked.

"If I knew what I was looking for—" Tabby left the sentence unfinished.

"*Maybe I could help,*" Beth said.

"Be my guest," Tabby said, trying to hand her magnifying glass to her friend.

"*Tabby. Please.*"

"Oh. Oops." Tabby smiled sheepishly. "Sorry. Forgot."

Beth leaned close to the table leg and peered at it through her filmy cloth. "*I do wish I could see clearly,*" she said softly. Finally, she sat up. "*I guess I'd better leave it to your living eyes. I can't see anything.*"

Tabby turned the leg to the next side and again put her glass to her eye. "Huh."

"*Find something?*" Beth asked.

"I'm not sure. But the carvings on this side seem—I don't know—deeper, somehow."

"*That sounds significant.*

Tabby pointed to a large rose at the top of the leg. "See? This is definitely carved deeper than the rest." She ran her fingers over it.

"*Whatever does it mean?*" Beth asked.

"Tabby!" Her mother called from the next room. "Dinner!"

Tabby sighed. "I guess we'll find out later." She set the table leg and her magnifying glass down on her bed. "I'd better go."

"*I'll talk to you later, then.*" Beth slid down through Tabby's floor.

Tabby stared at the spot where her friend had been. "That is so cool!" She hurried to the dining room.

"So what have you been up to today?" Her dad asked as he passed around a platter of steaks.

Tabby stabbed a large one. "Well, April and I went into town again."

"You've gotten to be pretty good friends with April, haven't you?"

Tabby nodded. "Yeah, I really like her. She's always ready for anything and she's lots of fun, too."

"It's funny, because she must be about sixty years older than you," her mother said.

Tabby shrugged. "I don't really notice any more. I'm also getting to be friends with—" she sucked in her breath and swallowed hard.

"Who?" her parents asked together.

"Umm—Jana."

"You know when we first came here, I thought Jana was going to cause no end of trouble," her dad said. "But she has turned out to be the best Assistant Manager I've ever had."

Tabby looked at him. "She really likes you, too, Dad. She was pretty mad when they hired you. But she says your lots smarter than she is."

Her father laughed. "You heard it here first, folks!"

Tabby's mom laughed with him. "Well, it is a relief to know. Though I can't imagine anyone not getting along with you, hon."

Her dad squeezed her mom's hand. "Thanks, hon." He turned back to Tabby. "So where were we when we got side-tracked onto me?"

Tabby swallowed a bite of steak and mashed potato. "April and I went into town."

"Oh, yes." Her dad grinned. "And what did the two of you do?"

"Well, first we explored the attics of the senior's home. Then we went over to an antique shop."

"Is there an antique shop?" her mother asked, her eyes sparkling.

Tabby wrinkled her nose. "Yeah. There was lots of junk there."

"One man's junk…"

Her father rolled his eyes. "So did you find anything interesting?"

Tabby reached for the buttered carrots. "We think we found the trunk belonging to that guy who fainted after seeing the ghost."

"Really?" Her mom leaned closer.

"Yeah. There were a bunch of letters and stuff from 1951. Along with all of his dirty laundry. And something weird at the very bottom of the trunk—a table leg."

"A table leg?" Her dad frowned.

"Yeah. It was pretty strange, so the owner told me I could bring it home to look at."

"Is that the table leg that was sitting on your bed?" her mom asked.

"Umm—yes."

She laughed. "I just realized what a silly question that was."

"Bring it in here, Tabs, and let's have a look," her dad suggested.

Tabby hurried to her room and brought the leg back. Then she laid it in front of her father who picked it up and looked at it closely.

"See. Here the carvings are different." Tabby pointed.

"Yes. I see." Her dad rubbed his fingers over them. Finally, he handed the leg back to Tabby. "Any ideas?"

"I don't—wait a moment!" Tabby took her steak knife and pressed it gently into the carving, then tried to pry at it.

It moved.

"I was right. It moved!" she said excitedly.

Her dad touched her arm. "Be careful."

Tabby worked the knife tip a little deeper into the crease and pried up again and suddenly, the entire rose popped out into her hand.

"Dad!" She held it up.

Her dad reached for it, turning it over in his hands. Then he looked back at the table leg. "Is there anything underneath?"

Tabby peered into the little hole that remained. "It's hollow. And there's a—space running up the centre of the leg."

She pushed her finger inside. "I feel something!" She frowned. "Like—paper—"

"Can you get it out?" her dad got to his feet and was now peering over her shoulder.

"I—don't—"

"Wait. Let me get some tweezers!" her mother said, bouncing to her feet and disappearing into her office. In a moment she was back and handed Tabby a pair of long-nosed tweezers. "These might help."

Tabby reached into the space and finally managed to grab a corner of a sheet of paper.

She pulled it out carefully and straightened it on the table. "It's a letter."

"Read it," her dad said.

Tabby frowned. *"Your daughter will be returned to you safe and sound as soon as I have the money. Put it in the canvas sack and throw it into the river under the bridge. Come alone and make sure no one—NO ONE—follows. If you say anything to anyone, you will never see your daughter again."*

She looked at her parents. "Oh. So— not a letter."

"Do you suppose it's a real ransom note?" her mother asked breathlessly.

"No." Her dad shook his head. "How can it be? Was there ever a kidnapping in this area?"

Her mom frowned. "Not that anyone has mentioned."

"And if there had been, it would have remained front page news forever," her dad said practically.

"But to be hidden like this." Her mom pulled the sheet of paper closer. "Someone didn't want this found. My, it sure is beautifully printed."

Tabby picked up the tweezers and started probing again. This time, she pulled out two more pieces of paper. She peered into the compartment.

"I think that's everything."

Her parents had already smoothed out the other two sheets of paper.

"This one's similar to the first," her mother said, "except that the drop point is different."

"Let me see," Tabby said. "Huh. This one says to drop the money into the garbage can in the town square."

"What does the third one say?" her dad asked.

Tabby leaned over it.

Your daughter is sitting in the railroad station in Essex.

Her dad sat back. "Well, someone sure had it figured out."

"The drop. The return."

As Tabby's mom ran her fingers over the third note, her eyes filled with tears. "I can only imagine what those parents must have gone through."

Tabby's dad slid an arm around her mother's shoulders. "Rose, dear, we don't even know if this was real."

Tabby's mom looked at her dad. "It was real, David," she said softly. "Somehow, I know it was real."

Chapter 12: Kidnapping. Or—Do I Just Have a Really Good Imagination?

A short time later, Tabby and her parents were crowded into April and Walt's little living room.

"Tabby discovered something quite extraordinary," her dad said, "And we just wanted to ask you two about it."

He laid the sheets of paper down in front of April and Walt.

April touched them. "You found these inside that table leg?"

Tabby nodded. "Yeah. There was a carving of a rose that popped out. In the space inside, we found these three pieces of paper."

Walt and April examined all three notes carefully.

Then Walt read, *"Your daughter will be returned to you safe and sound as soon as I have the money."*

He lifted his head. "Obviously, this is a second note. There had already been at least one."

"Why do you say that?" Tabby looked down at the note.

"Because there is no amount. It just says 'the money'."

"Huh. We never noticed that," her dad said.

"I think there was a real crime committed here," April said. "But something happened and the rest of the notes were never delivered."

"I agree." Tabby's mom nodded. "I think that someone started out on a kidnapping but, for whatever reason, never finished."

April looked at her. "But had they already kidnapped—?"

"I guess we'll never know." Tabby's dad shook his head.

"Oh, the poor parents!" April put her hands to her face. "The poor child!"

"Now, dear, we don't know anything," Walt said, patting his wife's arm.

April gave an unladylike snort. "Well, why else would someone do this? For fun? They obviously took some time." She held up the last note. "These were very carefully printed out. And stored with equal care where no one would find them."

Her husband nodded. Then shuffled the three pages, examining each one in turn. "I'd say this is fairly expensive paper."

April snapped plump fingers. "I'll be right back!" She disappeared through the doorway into the kitchen.

A moment later, she was back, carrying a sheet of paper. "Look! I was right. It is the same kind of paper as this letter we found in the trunk!"

Tabby leaned closer. "I think you're right."

April nodded. "See? It matches the writing on that letter as well." She handed the letter around to the others.

Walt agreed. "I think the printing was done with a fountain pen. Quite common in the early fifties."

"I've never used one, but I've seen them," Tabby's dad said.

Tabby looked around. "I don't even know what they are."

"They were pens that used tubes of ink," her mother told her. "With a nib similar to a calligraphy pen."

"Oh."

"The leg was also found in that man's trunk," April said.

"Mike Plunkett," Tabby said. "Who disappeared after the ghost was sighted." She looked at Walt. "Did you know him?"

Walt shook his head. "Knew *of* him. But if I remember correctly, he's one of the men who kept mostly to himself."

"So this Mike Plunkett must have been mixed up in a kidnapping," Tabby's mom said.

Her dad snorted. "Unless someone *else* was trying to hide some evidence. In Mike's trunk. With Mike's writing."

"Doesn't seem likely," Walt said.

"If only we could find out how the table leg got into the trunk," April said.

Tabby looked at her. "Maybe Ted could help."

Walt shrugged. "Well, it's certainly worth asking him."

The whole group walked over to the senior's home, then stood back while Walt rang the bell.

A woman came to the door. For a moment, she stared through the screen at the group gathered there. "What can I help you with?" she said finally, pushing the screen open.

"We'd like to talk to Ted, if he's available," Walt said.

She smiled. "I'll see what he's up to. Please, take a seat." She waved a hand toward the chairs on the sunny porch.

Tabby and her parents squeezed into the glider while Walt and April took chairs beside them.

"Well, this is a nice surprise," Ted said as he wheeled himself out the front door. "I didn't expect a visit quite this soon!" He shook hands with April and Walt.

"You remember Tabby," Walt said.

Ted grinned his toothless grin and nodded at Tabby. "How can I forget her? And I'm assuming these are your parents?"

"Yes. My dad, David and my mom, Rose."

"Very nice to meet you." Ted shook their hands. He looked around. "Well, with this many people here, I can only assume that something important has happened."

Walk cleared his throat. "That would be right. And we have a lot to tell you. But first, we want to ask you about the stuff you moved out of that man's room that day."

Ted frowned. "I'm glad to tell you what I can remember. But I don't know if there's much more."

"Do you remember a washstand in the room?"

Ted pursed his lips and frowned thoughtfully. Then his face cleared. "Now you mention it, I do. Big old marble-topped atrocity. Mrs. F wanted it gone. It took four of us to get it up to the attic."

"Do you remember if it was missing a leg?" April asked.

"Sure do. The leg fell off just as we lifted it. None of us were about to drop what we were doing to retrieve it, though. We just threw the leg in with the other junk."

Everyone looked at each other excitedly.

"Then that means—!" Tabby began.

Her dad put a hand on her shoulder. "All it means is that the leg was in the room of this mysterious Mike."

Ted slapped his leg. "Mike! That was his name! Imagine forgetting that one!"

Walt grinned.

"But it means that Mike is our man!" Tabby said. "He must be the one who wrote the notes!"

Ted's eyebrows went up. "Notes?"

"Maybe we should fill you in." April looked at Tabby. "It's Tabby's story. We'll let her tell it."

Tabby quickly brought him up to date, then showed him the notes and the unfinished letter.

Ted sat back. "Wow! That is something. A kidnapping!"

Tabby's dad was watching him. "Did you ever hear about a kidnapping here?"

Ted shook his head. "Never."

"Well, maybe it happened somewhere else," April said.

"But the washstand was here," Walt pointed out. "Unless Mike carried those notes with him when he moved here. But what would be the point of that?"

"Yeah. If you weren't going to go through with it, why wouldn't you just destroy the notes?" Tabby's mom said.

"So it had to be something he was planning here," Walt said.

"And started to carry out," her dad added.

"But with whom?" April said.

Chapter 13: In Which Mr. Withers Finally Tells His Story. And Proves He's Not Just a Grouch.

Tabby and her parents talked a while longer with Walt, April and Ted, then headed home.

Her dad sank down onto the couch in their apartment with a sigh. "Well, the only other person I know who was here during that time was Mr. Withers. So I'm going to talk to him about it."

"But I'd like to be there," Tabby said.

Her mom looked at her dad. "It *is* her mystery."

Her dad smiled. "How about if I invite him here?"

"That would be perfect," Tabby said.

He sighed. "I don't know how easy it will be. I've invited him over to dinner several times, and he's simply refused."

"Well, tell him there's something your family would like to discuss with him," her mom said. "He can't turn that down."

Her dad smiled. "Actually he can, but I'll try."

* * *

A few hours later, Mr. Withers was standing, rather nervously, in their front room.

"Thank you for joining us, Mr. Withers," Tabby's dad said.

He nodded slightly. "You said it was something important. I'm here."

Her dad cleared his throat. "Actually, Mr. Withers, it is my daughter, Tabby's story."

"Tabby?" Mr. Withers turned and stared at her. "Is it more about the ghost?"

Tabby swallowed. "Well, yes, it is. But it's turned into a mystery and we're hoping you can help."

Mr. Withers nodded and waited.

"We've found out a bit about the first day the ghost was sighted," she said.

Mr. Withers waved a hand dismissively. "Yes. I know all about that. The men were singing and the ghost appeared."

"Yes, but one of them was a bit more upset by the sight," her dad put in.

"Yes." Tabby nodded eagerly. "One of the men, Mike, fainted and had to go to the hospital. He never returned. Not even to collect his things."

Mr. Withers shrugged. "Several people quit that day. This—Mike?—was no different."

"Actually, we think he was," her dad said.

Mr. Withers looked at him.

"We think he had more reason than the rest to disappear," he went on.

"We think he was planning a kidnapping," Tabby said. "Or had already started to carry it out." She laid the three pieces of paper on the table in front of Mr. Withers.

He pulled off his glasses and gave them a quick polish, then shoved them back on. Then he looked down at the papers on the table. And froze.

"Mr. Withers?"

The elderly man had turned quite white. "Aggie!" he cried, sinking down into one of the chairs. Then he slumped over onto the table.

"Mr. Withers!" Tabby's dad sprang to his feet. "Quick, Rose, call 911! Mr. Withers has fainted!"

* * *

Within minutes, two uniformed men with a stretcher and a cartload of equipment were at the door.

By this time, Mr. Withers had regained consciousness, and stoutly refused to get on their stretcher and go with them.

"But, sir," one of them said. "I think we need to get you to the hospital as quickly as possible!"

"Nonsense! I just fainted. I'm not dying!"

The two paramedics looked at each other. One of them tried again. "But sir, a man your age--"

He got no further.

"A man my age would certainly know if there is any reason to panic!" Mr. Withers voice was rising.

"Yes, sir," the paramedic said meekly.

The other shrugged. "Well, your vitals seem to be all right."

"And they are," Mr. Withers said. "You might as well pack up your gear, gentlemen because I'm not going!"

"Well, it's your call. But you will be getting the bill, whether you go or not."

"I understand."

The two men shook their heads, but finally piled their gear onto the stretcher and pulled it out into the hall. "I hope you know what you're doing, sir," one of them said.

Tabby closed the door behind them and returned to the front room, where Mr. Withers was stretched comfortably on the couch.

"Now." Mr. Withers took a deep breath. "What was it you were telling me?"

Her dad looked at the elderly man. "Are you sure you're up to it?"

Mr. Withers pushed himself to a sitting position. "Believe me, after 60 years, I'm up to it."

"What?"

"Let's let your daughter tell her story first," Mr. Withers said.

Tabby looked at her dad, who nodded. "Ummm--so we found these papers." She retrieved them from the table.

Mr. Withers put out his hand and she handed them to him. He read each of them carefully. Then went back to the first and started again.

Suddenly, Tabby saw a tear trickle down his face.

He wiped at it with shaking fingers and shook his head. "After all this time—"

"Sorry?" Tabby's dad said.

"Go on." Mr. Withers nodded to Tabby.

Tabby nodded. "Well, we found a man who had cleaned out Mike's room after he disappeared. Then April and I managed to find the trunk he stuffed everything into."

"You've been busy," Mr. Withers said.

"And in that trunk was this." Tabby laid the table leg on the couch beside Mr. Withers who picked it up and examined it.

"The little rose carving on the one side comes out," Tabby told him, pointing. "That's where we found these papers."

"So you think it was this Mike who—" Mr. Withers lips quivered and he pressed them tightly together.

"We're pretty sure of it," her dad said. "The washstand this leg belongs to was in his room. The leg was packed into his trunk when his room was cleared out. We don't think it's been touched from that day till now."

Mr. Withers sighed and laid his head against the back of the couch.

"Are you all right, sir?" her father asked.

He nodded slightly, but continued to stare upwards. Finally, he sighed again. "I'm fine." He sat up. "Your reasoning is sound. Now I will tell you the rest."

He rubbed one hand over his face. "But I will have to go back a bit." Taking a deep breath, he started in, "My wife Agatha and I had dreamed of owning a hotel. We sold my family ranch, bought this land, and moved ourselves and our little daughter here. Then started to build."

He gave a half-smile. "Everything went well. Our plans were coming together beautifully."

He turned his head and looked toward the window. "I had a partner, Bill. Nicest man you'd ever want to meet. We'd been friends since we were in the fifth grade. But a few months before the hotel was due to open, Bill lost all of his money in an investment scheme. I tried to convince him to stay on as a partner, but he wouldn't even hear about it. Finally, the only thing I was able to convince him to do was to stay on as a foreman."

Mr. Withers looked at us. "I couldn't just turn him out into the world with nothing." Then he frowned. "But then he betrayed me." He glanced at the papers in his hand. "Or at least I thought he had."

He was silent for a moment. Then he sighed and went on. "Early one morning, just a short time before the hotel was due to open, I found a note in the centre of my desk." He pulled out his wallet and opened it, removing a small, plastic pouch. From the pouch, he carefully withdrew a much-folded and fragile piece of paper. Gently, he spread it out. "This note."

Tabby and her parents leaned over it.

It was faded and old, and starting to come apart in some of the seams, but still fairly legible.

"I have your daughter." Tabby read, *"She will be returned to you for the sum of fifty thousand dollars. If you tell anyone— ANYONE—you will never see her again. You will receive further instructions."*

She looked at Mr. Withers. "So it's true." The she gasped and clapped a hand over her mouth and stared at him, wide-eyed. She lowered her hand. "And it was your—" She swallowed hard.

Mr. Withers nodded and wiped at another tear.

Tabby's mother handed him a tissue.

"It was my little Aggie." He crossed both arms before him and placing gnarled hands on his chest. "My little song-bird. I ran to our suite, but, of course, she was gone. I don't know how they got into her room, but she had obviously been taken in the night. The only clothing missing was her little—night dress." He gasped and sobbed aloud.

Tabby's mom, tears streaming down her own face, handed him several more tissues.

Sometime later, he wiped his eyes and blew his nose. "I didn't even dare tell my wife. The note said not to tell anyone."

He shook his head. "I was so sure she would be returned," he said softly. He blinked more tears away. "I went immediately and got the money from the bank in Essex. It wasn't that difficult because I was always withdrawing different amounts to pay for construction costs. Then I waited."

He looked at Tabby's dad. "To say it was the worst day of my life, would be a complete understatement. I don't remember much of what I did. I vaguely remember shouting at people. The hotel was in an uproar over the ghost sighting and my wife kept asking me where our little Aggie was. I felt like I was slowly going insane."

"My friend, Bill, never showed up to work that morning. No one had seen him. I don't know when I began to suspect him. Sometime during the day, I guess. It occurred to me that Bill had just lost all of his money. Perhaps a kidnapping—"

"You fired him," her dad said. "When he didn't show."

"Did I?" Mr. Withers said, shrugging. "Probably. I did a lot of things. I watched and I waited all day, but no note ever arrived. I never heard from the kidnapper again."

His voice dropped to a whisper. "That night, my beloved wife fell off our balcony to her death." He scrubbed at his face and blew his nose. Then he looked again at Tabby's dad. "I had lost my entire family. Everything that was most important to me. In one day."

The room was silent for a few minutes as Mr. Withers sobbed aloud and the rest of them struggled to compose themselves.

Even Tabby had to wipe at her streaming tears.

Finally, Mr. Withers took a deep breath and blew his nose again. "I held desperately to the belief that at least Aggie would be returned to me. I still didn't dare tell anyone about her kidnapping for fear I would jeopardize that."

"And I never did. I finally made up a story about sending her to live with relatives. No one knew that Agatha and I had no other family."

"For several days, I lived in a dream world. I couldn't eat or sleep. Then a kind friend told me that the worst thing I could do was to allow grief to stop *me* from living. I realized that the one way I could remember my wife—my family—was to finish the dream we had begun. Even if Agatha couldn't be beside me to see it finished.

"So I did it. And waited for Aggie."

"The Hotel opened and I waited for Aggie. The years went past and still I waited for Aggie. I never once, though over sixty years have passed, allowed myself to give up the hope that one day, I would turn around and she'd be there."

He accepted another tissue from Tabby's mom. "I'm still waiting."

He laid his old, crumbling note with the others. "And now, after all these years, I know at least part of the story."

"It wasn't your friend, Bill, after all," Tabby said. "But this—Mike."

Mr. Withers nodded. "That seems to be so."

"The same Mike who fainted when he saw the ghost," Tabby went on, thoughtfully.

Mr. Withers nodded again.

"The ghost," Tabby repeated. "The ghost who appeared— the next day." She frowned and shook her head. "It couldn't be that easy—" Suddenly, she jumped to her feet. "I've just thought of something!" she told her parents excitedly. "But we're going to need everyone!" She reached for the phone.

 Chapter 14: Where Tabby
makes an Important Discovery.
And Solves the case. Sort of...

Tabby called April and asked her and Walt to bring Ted to the hotel. She, her parents and Mr. Withers met them at the main door.

"Everyone follow me!" Tabby said, beckoning with one hand as she ran toward the darkened ballroom.

Several staff members, hearing the commotion, joined the group.

"We'll need all of the lights on," Tabby said.

April walked quickly to the wall and pressed switch after switch. Slowly the shadows in the great room disappeared.

"Now, Ted, you told us you knew the exact spot where the ghost first appeared," Tabby said. "We need you to show us."

Ted moved his wheelchair to the centre of the room and spun around in a circle. "Well, I was about here," he said, moving to one corner of the room. "And Rolly was standing just there," he pointed. "And the ghost appeared right beside him." He rolled a few feet. "Right here."

Tabby looked at Mr. Withers. "Mr. Withers. How hard would it be to tear up the floor here?"

Mr. Withers stared at her. "Tear up the floor?"

"Yes. I think we're about to find the answers to a lot of questions," Tabby said. "But we need to see under the floor to tell for sure."

"Tabs, honey, we can't just go tearing up floors," her father said.

"I will donate all of my allowance to having it fixed if I'm wrong. Four hundred and seventeen dollars and fifty eight cents."

Her father looked at Mr. Withers, who shrugged.

"Well, I, for one would like to see what's under there," April said.

"I'd be happy to do it," Walt added. "I'll even pay for the repairs."

"What do you say, Mr. Withers?" Tabby's dad said.

"If it might clear up this mystery, and if the man who originally installed the floor is willing to fix it afterwards, I say let's do it." Mr. Withers nodded.

Walt looked around. "Could someone bring me my tools out of my car trunk?" He waved a set of car keys.

Minutes later, he was kneeling on the floor, prying at the first board with a wood chisel. "Wow! This was here to stay! I do good work!"

A few of the people chuckled, but most were intent on what he was doing.

Finally, with the sound of splintering wood, he managed to pull the board up. The next came up a bit more easily. And the next and the next.

Finally, he had pulled all of the hardwood boards from a four-foot patch, revealing the planks beneath. "Now I need someone to plug in this saw," he said, holding up an electrical cord.

One of the staff ran off and returned a short time later with a long extension cord, which he plugged into a wall socket.

Tabby grabbed the cord and attached it to Walt's saw. "There." She knelt beside him.

"Not too close, Kitten," April said. "Power tools, you know."

Tabby smiled at her. "I'll be careful."

Walt flipped the switch and the saw screamed into life. Then he lowered the blade down and it began to bite into the wood. Carefully, he slid the saw along the floor, cutting through the boards in one direction. Then he turned and cut another line perpendicular to the first. Then he turned again. Finally, he finished a fourth cut that brought him back to where he had started.

He set the saw down. "Someone want to help me with this?"

He pushed the edge of his chisel into one of the cuts and pried upwards. The chunk of floor lifted an inch or so.

He pushed the chisel deeper and tried again. This time, he was able to lift it enough that two of the men could get their fingers underneath and lift.

The whole section came up with a groan and the sound of cracking wood.

They flipped it back and laid it on the floor nearby and the group crowded closer and peered into the disclosed cavity.

There was a collective gasp.

"What is it?" someone asked.

"It seems to be some—old cloth," someone else said.

"*May I see?*" a small, clear voice said.

Everyone spun around.

A small, veiled figure was standing just outside the group.

Someone screamed and then there was a great scramble as everyone backed up.

Even Tabby's parents and friends moved away, April pulling Ted's wheelchair before her as she edged backwards.

Soon only Tabby and the ghost remained in the centre of the brightly lit ballroom.

Beth drew closer to the hole in the floor. Then stopped beside it and leaned forward, peering inside.

Tabby joined her. "What do you think, Beth?" she asked.

Beth shrugged.

"Well, let's see if we can find out more," Tabby said. Gingerly, she reached into the space and pulled at the cloth.

"I don't know if we should touch anything," her mother's voice cautioned.

Tabby looked up. Her parents and friends had returned, huddled close together on the opposite side of the gaping hole from her and Beth, their eyes darting back and forth uncertainly between the two of them.

"I'll just lift it a tiny bit," Tabby said. The cloth shredded apart. She gasped as a small, skeletal face was uncovered. A few strands of long, blond hair still clung to it.

At the same time, the veil suddenly fell from the ghost's face. A young girl with long, blonde hair was revealed. Transparent hands slowly reached up and touched transparent cheeks.

Now all eyes were riveted on her.

She held her hands out and looked at them, turning them so she could see the palms, then the backs.

Finally, she looked down at the little huddled figure so long hidden under the floorboards. *"It's me,"* she said softly. *"After all this time, you finally found me."* Suddenly, she turned and looked at Tabby. *"I remember!"* she whispered.

"So this is where your body has been buried all these years," Tabby said.

Beth nodded. *"Yes."*

"Beth," Tabby said. "What else do you remember?"

"Beth?" her mother said. "Tabby, do you know this— person?"

Tabby looked at her parents. "We've been working together on the puzzle for a couple of weeks. I promised not to tell anyone."

"Not even your parents?" her dad said.

"I'm sorry, Dad, but I did make a promise."

"We'll talk about it later," her mother said, frowning.

Tabby turned back to Beth. "What else do you remember, Beth?" she asked again.

Beth looked at Tabby, her smile fading. *"This is where he put me!"*

"Can you tell us about it?" Tabby asked.

"I can." Beth pressed faint hands together. *"At last, I can."* She turned to face the silent group. *"I lived in this hotel. I had been asleep and this man came. I woke up just as he pressed something over my nose and mouth. A cloth. It smelled funny. I must have gone back to sleep because suddenly, I woke up again. I didn't know what was happening for a moment. Someone was carrying me. Finally, I looked around and recognized the hotel lobby. I screamed."*

"Someone else—a man—shouted, and the person carrying me turned and hurried into the ballroom. I started to struggle and screamed again. He put his hands on my throat and I couldn't breathe. Then, suddenly, I was standing beside him, looking down at him and the girl lying on the floor at his feet. He stood up and

110

moved into the shadows just as another man came running into the room. Bill. My father's friend. He knelt down beside the girl."

"Your *father's* friend?" another voice asked. Tabby looked up to see that Mr. Withers had also joined them. He moved slowly closer to Beth on uncertain legs.

"*My father's friend*," she repeated.

"Oh!" Mr. Withers stared at her. Looked into her face for the first time. Then he sank to the floor.

Walt and April gathered around him. "Sir? Sir, are you all right?"

"I'm fine!" he waved them away. "I'm fine. Just let me catch my breath!" He stared up at Beth.

Tabby stepped a little closer. "So then what happened?"

"*The man who had been carrying me grabbed a hammer and hit Bill and Bill fell down. Then the man pulled him out of the room. I waited beside the girl on the floor and a while later, the man came back. By this time, it was starting to get light outside. I could see the sun coming up through the windows of the ballroom.*

"*The draperies hadn't been hung up yet. They were still in boxes stacked to one side of the ballroom. The man pried one open and pulled out one of the filmy drapes. He wiped up something that had spilled on the floor when he had pulled Bill out of the room, then wrapped the girl in the curtain and picked her up. Then he stopped and listened.*"

"*We could hear the bus coming. The bus that the workers rode every morning.*

"*The man ran to the side of the ballroom, where the floor hadn't been finished yet. He pushed the girl down into the space under the floor and placed several planks of wood over her.*

"*Then he started to nail things down, using the same hammer he had hit Bill with.*

"*By the time the rest of the workers came into the room, the girl was completely hidden under the floor.*

"*And that's when I forgot.*"

"Do you remember—me?" Mr. Withers said hoarsely.

Beth turned to him and frowned. She tilted her head to one side and peered into his face. "*Papa?*" she said, finally.

"Aggie? Is it really you? After all this time?"

"*Aggie*." The ghost paused, frowning. "*Yes*," she said at last. Suddenly, her face lit up in a smile. "*Oh, Papa! It is me! It is!*"

Mr. Withers began to cry. He put his hands over his face and sobbed.

Aggie moved closer to him and, putting out one transparent hand, stroked his head. "*Don't cry, Papa,*" she said softly. "*Don't cry. It's all right now.*"

"After all this time," Mr. Withers choked. "And I—thought—"

"*Everything's all right now,*" Aggie said. She looked around and smiled. "*Everything's all right.*"

For several minutes, everyone stood silently while Mr. Withers cried and Aggie continued to stroke his white head with a ghostly hand.

Finally, Tabby moved closer to her. "So your name is Aggie?"

Aggie turned to her. "*Yes. I was named after my mother, Agatha.*"

"Well, I'm going to take a while to get used to that," Tabby said. "I hope you don't mind if I make a few mistakes in the beginning."

Aggie looked at Tabby sadly. "*I'm sorry, my good, good friend Tabby, but I don't think we will be allowed any further time together.*"

"What?" Tabby said loudly. "Why not?"

Aggie smiled. "*I was given time and opportunity to finish what had been started. But now it's time for me to go. There are others waiting for me.*"

"Your mom?" Tabby asked.

"*Yes,*" Aggie said. Suddenly she pressed transparent hands to her cheeks. "*Mama!*"

"What is it, Be-Aggie?" Tabby said.

"*I followed her. I didn't know who she was when I saw her. But I felt—drawn to her. I followed her to her rooms.*" She looked at her father. "*Papa, I'm sorry!*"

He stared at her. "What are you saying, Aggie?"

"*I frightened her. She fell. I remember it all now.*" She covered her face with her hands. "*Oh, how I wish I did not.*"

"Are you telling me that you tried to talk to your mother and that she fell?"

"*She backed away from me and— Oh, Papa, I'm so sorry!*"

Mr. Withers took a deep breath. "So now I know it all," he said softly. He shook his head and buried it in his hands once more.

Aggie reached out and touched him again. "*I'm so sorry, Papa,*" she whispered.

He lifted a tear-streaked face and looked at her. "It wasn't your fault, baby. You weren't responsible for what was done to you. And how could you know what would happen? You were only seeking help!"

Aggie was silent a moment, one ghostly hand on her father's head. Finally, she nodded. "*I must go to her,*" she said. "*I must explain.*"

"Now?" Tabby asked.

"*Now,*" Aggie said. "*She has waited a long time.*" She looked at Tabby. "*Thank you Tabby Pillay. I knew when I first saw you that you were the one to help me. And you did.*"

"I've always liked mysteries," Tabby said. "Of course, none of them have been quite this exciting or—personal before."

"*Well, I am grateful,*" Aggie said. She looked down at her father. "*Papa?*"

Mr. Withers looked up at her.

"*Papa, I have to leave now.*"

He got to his feet. "Oh, my little girl, so soon?" he said, clasping both hands to his chest. "I just got you back!"

Aggie smiled at him. "*I won't be far, Papa.*"

He nodded. Made a slight reaching motion toward her with one hand, then dropped that hand to his side.

"*Take care of me, Papa.*" She glanced down at the small body still lying quietly under the floor.

"I will, baby. I'll take special care," her father said.

"*Good-bye.*" The filmy figure melted away.

"Good-bye, my sweetheart!" Mr. Withers again sank to the floor, his hands lying loosely beside him.

"Mr. Withers, are you all right?" Tabby's dad moved closer and put one hand on his boss' shoulder.

"I'm fine, David," Mr. Withers said, his eyes brimming with tears. "For the first time in sixty years, I'm . . . fine."

* * *

"So all this time, you had been talking to the ghost and you never told us a thing!" Tabby's mother was just a bit upset.

"I promised her, Mom." Tabby grasped her mom's hand and squeezed it. "She didn't want me to tell anyone else."

"But why not? We could have helped."

"I've been thinking about that. And I think it was because the last adult she was with killed her. And hid her body." She looked at her mom. "She didn't trust anyone any more."

"But she couldn't remember."

"Well, maybe not remember exactly, but she could still have a feeling. Anyways, I'm just guessing."

"And that's another thing," her mom said. "Why couldn't she remember? Even when we uncovered the body, she didn't remember anything until the cloth was removed from her face."

"April was talking about that," Tabby said. "She said the cloth that Mike had used was pure silk. And that there is something about pure materials, especially silk, that stops or insulates against anything supernatural."

"Sounds like hokum to me!" Her dad grinned.

"Well, you have to admit that she wasn't able to remember at all until the cloth was removed," Tabby's mom said.

"I don't have to admit anything." Her dad's grin widened.

Tabby sighed. "So, all of this time, Mr. Withers thought his best friend had kidnapped his daughter and disappeared with her."

"What a terrible thing to carry around," her mom said.

Her dad put an arm around her mother's shoulders. "Next to the fact that your wife has just died, I guess so."

"I can't imagine his pain," her mom said, unhappily.

Tabby sat down. "Well, I probably shouldn't say this, but I'm a bit sad that everything has been explained."

"Not everything." Her mom looked at Tabby then at her husband. "We still don't know what Mike did with Bill's body. Or what happened to Mike."

"Mike most likely dragged Bill's body down to the river and dumped it in," her dad said. "As for what happened to him? Well, everything had gone wrong with his plan. I think he was just putting as many miles between himself and the crime scene as he could."

Her mom nodded. "Probably changed his name and started over."

Her dad pursed his lips. "Good guess."

"But I'm surprised no one ever found Bill's body," her mom said. "Wouldn't it have emerged at some point?"

Her dad shrugged. "We're only a few miles from the ocean. It could easily have disappeared once it reached there."

"Well, I'm glad, for Mr. Withers' sake—and for Aggie's, that we were able to figure out what happened," Tabby said. "And, like I said, I'm a bit sad to have it all done." She looked thoughtful. "Still—"

"What." Her mother was looking at her.

Tabby shrugged.

"Tabs, I know that look. What are you up to?"

"I was just thinking that we still don't know anything about the 'other' ghosts."

Her dad stared at her. "What other ghosts?"

"Well, the one who was talking to Ms. Bennett just before she fell. Maybe the one who *caused* her fall. And others."

"You mean we have other ghosts in this hotel?" her mother said.

"That's what Aggie said."

"That's it. I'm leaving!" Her mother grinned.

Tabby's dad looked at her mom. "Are you kidding? We couldn't pry you out of this hotel with a crowbar!"

Her mom laughed.

"Or me either!" Tabby grinned at her parents. "You know what? I think I've finally decided—I like it here!"

Discussion Questions:

1. Why did Tabby's dad get the job at the Overlook Hotel?
2. How would you react if you saw what Tabby saw when her parents were dancing?
3. Why did Aggie feel drawn to Tabby?
4. Spirits who remain are said to have 'unfinished business'. What was Aggie's?
5. How old would Aggie be if she had lived?
6. Why was Aggie's first appearance in the ballroom?
7. What is the punishment for kidnapping?
8. Why was Mr. Withers so grumpy all the time?
9. Have you ever been friends with someone who wasn't your age?
10. How do we know there are other spirits in the hotel?

About the Author:

Photo Credit: David Handschuh

Born on a ranch in Southern Alberta and raised by a family of writers, Diane Stringam Tolley caught the bug early, publishing her first story at the age of 11. Trained in Journalism, she has written countless novels, articles, short stories, plays, songs and poems. Her Christmas books, Carving Angels and Kris Kringle's Magic have become perennial family favourites.

Tolley and her Husband live in Northern Alberta and are the parents to six and grandparents to seventeen.

If you enjoyed Ghost of the Overlook,
You might also enjoy these books
by the same author.
Available online:

Essence
Essence: A Second Dose
Carving Angels
(Kris Kringles) Magic
Gnome for Christmas
SnowMan
Words
High Water

Find me at:
https://twitter.com/StoryTolley
https://www.facebook.com/diane.tolley1
Blog: http://dlt-lifeonthreranch.blogspot.ca
Web Site: http:// dianestringamtolley.com

I'd love to hear from you!
dtolley@shaw.ca

Made in the USA
Charleston, SC
05 November 2016